JOHNNY BALL
UNDERCOVER FOOTBALL GENIUS

MATT OLDFIELD

ILLUSTRATED BY TIM WESSON

WALKER BOOKS

JOHNNY BALL

To Iona and Isla, readers steadfast and new – M.O.

First published 2021 by Walker Books Ltd
87 Vauxhall Walk, London SE11 5HJ

2 4 6 8 10 9 7 5 3 1

Text © 2021 Matt Oldfield
Illustrations © 2021 Tim Wesson

The right of Matt Oldfield and Tim Wesson to be identified as author
and illustrator respectively of this work has been asserted by them in
accordance with the Copyright, Designs and Patents Act 1988

This book has been typeset in Century Gothic

Printed and bound by CPI Group (UK) Ltd, Croydon CR0 4YY

British Library Cataloguing in Publication Data:
a catalogue record for this book is available from the British Library

ISBN 978-1-4063-9127-5

www.walker.co.uk

MIX
Paper from
responsible sources
FSC® C020471

CHAPTER 1

FUTURE NUMBER ONE FOOTBALL GENIUS

I'M BACK! I've got loads of exciting stuff to tell you...

But before I do, just in case you somehow missed the amazing tale of how I became an ACCIDENTAL FOOTBALL GENIUS (come on, where have you been?!), my name is Johnny Ball and I LOVE football.

BUT ... and it's a big but, or as Dad likes to say "the greatest BUT since Scratchy Bottom". (It's a real place, I promise. Daniel and I googled it once and it really exists!) I'm not that great at playing football.

There's another BIG BUT... Despite that, my incredible football ideas have got me the job of assistant manager for the Tissbury Tigers!

Now, if you're a new fan, you're probably wondering, "Blimey, how did you become the assistant manager of the Tissbury Tigers? They sound like a top team and, well, you're only nine-and-a-quarter years old!"

NAME: Johnny Ball (nope, no terrible middle name to see here, folks)
AGE: 9¼
HOME: Tissbury, the best town in the world
BEST FRIEND: Tabia, the best best friend in the world
FAMILY: Football-CRAAAAAAAZY! You'll see...
FAVOURITE THING EVER: Football, duh!
WEAKNESSES: Not THAT good at football (definitely CAN KICK IT, though, despite what some people say)
STRENGTHS: Really great football ideas (look out for my light-bulb moments – *TING!*)
NEW JOB: Assistant manager of the Tissbury Tigers!

I know, it's pretty hard to believe, isn't it? But it's true, I promise, and to prove it, here's the story straight from *The Tissbury Times* (don't worry, you can keep this copy – I've got eight more in my Greatest Football Moments folder, plus one up on my bedroom wall):

BURY TIMES ✢

JOHNNY'S ON THE BALL!
TISSBURY PRIMARY WIN THE COUNTY CUP, THANKS TO THEIR YOUNG FOOTBALL GENIUS

Yesterday afternoon, Tissbury Primary lifted the County Cup trophy for the first time in five years, after defeating Epic Forest 2–1 in a hard-fought final. Tabia Haddad and Billy Newland scored the goals for Tissbury, but the true hero of the hour was their young man(ager) with a plan, Johnny Ball, brother of Tissbury Tigers superstar, Daniel. Filling in for the team's usual coach, Martin Mann, the 9-year-old showed off his great football ideas to pull off a sensational cup upset.

With time running out and Epic Forest on the front foot, Johnny entered the field himself and won the game for Tissbury with a devastating display of teamwork.

As Isabelle Johnstone dribbled the ball forward in the final minute of the match, her teammates formed a ferocious line of lions to protect her. Then, after a call from Johnny, the Tissbury players spread out to form a Flying T formation. The extraordinary scene left the Epic defence at sixes and sevens.

"Yeah, it was a pretty good idea, I guess," Newland said after scoring the winning goal, "but the best part was my absolute BANGER of a shot!"

Johnny's football genius has been on display throughout the tournament, leading Tissbury past more talented opponents and all the way to County Cup glory.

"My Johnny-boo has always been a smart little sausage," his mother, Elizabeth, told us proudly.

And Mrs Ball wasn't the only one impressed by her son's great ideas. "Johnny's got a brilliant football brain," proclaimed Tissbury Town manager, Paul Porterfield, who was there watching in the crowd. "If he can keep this up, he could be doing my job one day!"

So there you have it, the story of the number one proudest achievement of my entire life ... EVER! After that, I really didn't think things could get any better, but they did.

The Tissbury Tigers Under-15s manager, Chris Crawley, offered me the chance to be his new assistant. Well, I couldn't say no to that, could I?

Not if I wanted to be "THE NEXT PAUL PORTERFIELD"! He was not only the Tissbury Town manager but also probably the best manager in the whole wide world. This was my chance to follow in his brilliant brain-steps, and become the future number one football genius in the whole wide world.

But – and it's another big but (hehehe!) – there's just one problem... Tissbury Tigers' star player?

Daniel "The Cannon" Ball.

Or as I like to call him: my super-talented big brother.

ME coaching HIM?! Oh boy, things are about to get very, very interesting.

Trust me, my football manager adventure is only just getting started...

CHAPTER 2

DANNY'S "DEMANDZ"

"Do you think this winning feeling will ever get old?"
I asked Tabia as we walked home from school
together. It was now nearly a whole week since the
final, and we were still the talk of the town.

Tabia pretended to think about my question for a
millisecond (that's 1/1000 of a second by the way)
and then shook her head so hard that it made a
horrible *CRICK!* sound. "No way, *BOZO-BRAIN!*"

Nasty name battles – that was another thing that
would never get old.

"I hope you're right, *TURD-TAIL!*"

"I'm always right, *WEE-WHALE!*"

"Cool, that rhymed!"

I hoped Tabia was right about being right; she
usually was. It was super fun being a football hero
for once, rather than a football hopeless. Suddenly,
the really popular Year 6 kids were nodding at

me in the playground, and we even went out for a family meal that was ALL ABOUT ME! Talk about dining out on your success, eh?

But it wasn't all balloons and triple-decker burgers, and my best friend knew it.

"So, how are you feeling about coaching the Tigers, *PIG-PLANK?*" Tabia asked me, kicking a stone to make it sound super casual.

Ah yes, Johnny Ball: Tissbury Tigers Assistant Manager – the first day of my scary new job was creeping closer and closer, like a horrible stinky smell in the fridge. It was now just one day away.

"I … can't … wait," I lied, really, really badly.

Tabia turned, hands on hips like an angry adult. "The truth please, *TURTLE-TONGUE!*"

"They're big, they're talented, they're teenagers AND one of them is my brother. The truth is … I'd rather coach a whole safari of ACTUAL wild tigers than the Tissbury Tigers! What am I going to teach THEM about football, Tabs? How to not be that good?"

"Hey, you'll be brilliant," Tabia told me. "And don't worry, Coach Crawley will tell you what to do – that's his job. Just remember: JOHNNY BALL, YOU'RE A FOOTBALL GENIUS!"

"Thanks, Tabs, I guess we'll soon find out if that's true..."

When I got home that day, the house was super quiet. Mum and Dad were out in the garden, fixing the football goal for the millionth time, and Daniel was in his bedroom, probably listening to loud, angry music through his headphones.

"Perfect!" I thought. "Time to think." In order to impress Coach Crawley, I was going to need some really great football ideas, and fast. So I rushed upstairs to my room and opened my "JNB" pocket notebook with my initials on all the pages. I waited for the light-bulb moments to arrive...

Think, Johnny, think!

But before I could even write one word, Daniel barged his way into my bedroom without knocking.

"All right," he said, lifting his head like a seal trying to balance a ball on its nose.

"All right," I replied, trying to copy his cool-kid move.

It was a strong start to our conversation.

"So, I've been thinking, Bro..."

Uh-oh, my brother thinking was almost always a bad thing.

"...look, don't get me wrong, I'm proper buzzed about your sick wins with Tissbury Primary, and I'm calm that Coach Crawley asked you to come join the Tigers... BUT..."

I knew it. I knew there was going to be a great big BUT (hehehe!).

"...there's things you gotta understand. This ain't no County Cup clowning any more, J – this is serious. We ain't got time for no playground prankz!"

"I know, don't worry, I won't—" I tried to say, but Daniel wasn't done yet.

"Because here's the sitch: we've got six games left this season and if we flame them all, the Tigers will probs win the league title. You hear that? THE LEAGUE TITLE! We ain't won it for fifteen years, so we can't mess this up, gottit?"

"Gottit. You really don't need to worr—"

Nope, Daniel still wasn't done. "Seeing as we gotta be at training together from now on, I've got a few demandz, yeah, about the way it's gonna be. When it comes to football, no one makes a fool of me – you get me? So, that saddo scarf of yours has gotta go. I know Grandpa George gave it to you, but it makes you look like a melting snowman."

Harsh, but a tiny bit true.

"And don't do anything else embarrassing, OK? You know what I mean – dancing, singing, joking, trying to play football. That sorta thing. What else? Oh yeah, don't EVER try to coach ME. The other guys maybe, but leave me out. Right, one more and this is a real big deal – don't tell ANYONE that I'm your bro. Sweet, that's it, lil man – so, we cool?"

POP! My brother's "demandz" were the pin that finally burst my happy football bubble. Again! It was now his number two talent, after scoring lots and lots of great goals. No, we weren't "cool".

"Why don't you want the Tigers to know that we're brothers?" I asked.

It seemed like a simple question to me, but Daniel looked awkwardly down at the floor and kicked an imaginary ball a few times before answering. "Look, it's just easier that way, lil man – less chat, less stress. You can do your thing and I can do mine. Safe."

"But how? Surely the Tigers already know about me, anyway?"

SILENCE – that was a big fat "no" then. These days, Daniel never let me meet any of his friends, so they probably didn't even know he had a brother.

"Soz, that ain't my problem, lil man," he said eventually, with a shrug. "If you really still wanna come coach the Tigers, you'll just have to work it out. And no mole-ing on me to Mum and Dad, OK?"

I nodded glumly. Even though Daniel was my new number one least favourite person, I knew better than to try that nasty trick.

That night, when I went up to bed, I found a folded piece of paper on my pillow that looked like it had been torn out of a school exercise book. There was a letter scrawled pretty badly on the front: **J**.

I could only think of one person who was cool/ lazy enough to call me that:

Dear J,

Sick chat earlier. Here's a list of my demandz,
just to help you remember, innit.

1) Don't wear that saddo scarf
2) Don't do nothing else embarrassing either
3) Don't tell anyone that I'm your bro
4) I'll repeat it coz this one's well important:
Don't tell ANYONE that I'm your bro.
5) Don't EVER try to coach ME

See ya downstairs at breakfast,
Danny B

My brother was serious, so what was I going
to do? Well, my first angry thought was, "FINE,
WHATEVER, BRO, IF YOU DON'T WANT ME AROUND,
I'LL JUST GO BACK TO BEING THE TISSBURY PRIMARY
MANAGER THEN!"

I was going to miss all my friends in my old team
anyway, and it was waaaay easier telling nine-
year-olds what to do...

But then I remembered what Paul Porterfield had
said about me after we won the County Cup Final:
"Johnny's got a brilliant football brain. If he can

keep this up, he could be doing my job one day!"

Johnny Ball: Future Tissbury Town Manager – that was my number one football dream. To reach the top, I had to be brave and sometimes do things that seemed super scary. Like coaching teenagers and making my stupid big brother mad.

So, Daniel didn't want his teammates to know that I was his brother, eh? Fine, well I would just have to be: Johnny Ball: Undercover Football Genius!

CHAPTER 3

UNDERCOVER FOOTBALL GENIUS?

UNDERCOVER FOOTBALL GENIUS sounded super cool. I moved it straight to the top of the "Super-Cool Jobs" list in my head:

1) UNDERCOVER FOOTBALL GENIUS
2) TISSBURY TOWN CAPTAIN AND TOP SCORER
3) INTERNATIONAL ICE-CREAM TASTER
4) SPACE COWBOY
5) RECORD-BREAKING LEGO BUILDER.

At first, I was excited. Lucky me, I had just given myself the number one greatest job in the whole wide world! I was going to have the best time ever, and there was nothing that Daniel could do to stop me...

But then came the dreaded SECOND THOUGHTS:

Really, Johnny, are you sure about this?

What even is an "Undercover Football Genius"?

Did you make that job up just now? (The other ones on my list are real, though, obviously.)

All of the football geniuses I could think of – Paul Porterfield, Pelé, Johnny "The Rocket" Jeffries, Johan Cruyff – they were really famous and definitely NOT undercover. Hmm, I had some serious mind-mapping to do...

I don't know about you, but when I hear the word "undercover", the first things I see are:

UNDERCOVER LOOKS

FAKE MOUSTACHE

SPY SUNGLASSES

You're right, it would have been the perfect disguise if I was about to become a top-secret agent in Tokyo, but I wasn't – I was about to become an assistant football manager in Tissbury!

And for that, I would need to be able to talk without something tickling my top lip, and I would need to be able to see well during the daytime too. So I crossed out:

Fake ~~moustache~~

Spy ~~sunglasses~~.

Right, well what else could I use to help me go undercover with the Tissbury Tigers? I was going to need:

1. A NEW (FOOTBALL) LOOK

Sadly, as Johnny Ball: Undercover Football Genius, I wouldn't be able to wear my favourite red tracksuit any more. Because what if one of the Tigers recognised it from the County Cup Final or the photos in The Tissbury Times?

And Daniel had made it very clear that my super-long scarf was NOT allowed.

I needed an outfit that was going to make me look a bit older and also a bit less Ball-y...

A hat? My hair was way curlier than Daniel's, but it was exactly the same colour. "Football boot black," as Mum liked to call it. So, maybe it was best if I covered it up with something super stylish?

SUPER-STYLISH HAT 1   **SUPER-STYLISH HAT 2**

What about cowboy boots? As you probably know, teenagers don't like listening to 9-year-olds. But if I looked a bit taller and a bit more dangerous too, maybe they wouldn't laugh ... so much?

And a big belly? I have Mr Mann, the old Tissbury Primary manager, to thank for this one. It was my best idea yet because:

a) Everyone knows that bigger = older.

b) Hopefully it would mean that Coach Crawley would make me do less running around.

c) That way, I could still wear my super-long scarf, but ... UNDERCOVER!

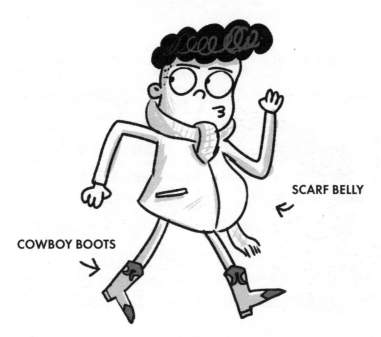

SCARF BELLY

COWBOY BOOTS

Right, that was my new look sorted! So I moved straight on to the second half of my undercover football genius plan:

2. A NEW (FOOTBALL) NAME

If Daniel and I were pretending not to be brothers, then we definitely couldn't have the same last name any more, could we? In fact, this was my chance to come up with a TOTALLY NEW NAME!

> *HI THERE, I'M … RAKEEM VAN DER RHINO!*

> *NICE TO MEET YOU. THE NAME'S PLATYPUS … PLATYPUS MURPHY!*

After a lot of thinking, I decided that actually maybe I should stick to my initials. That way, I could keep using my "JNB" pocket notebook. But what would my sort-of new name be?

TING! MINI LIGHT-BULB MOMENT. I had an idea. I ran downstairs and looked up at the really long shelves of our big family bookcase. It was a pretty awesome library, especially if you were interested in ... yep, you guessed it – FOOTBALL!

We had books about absolutely everything. You name it, we had it:

football fitness,

football history,

football recipes,

football travel,

even football crime fiction!

Normally, it took me ages to pick the best one, but this time I knew what I was looking for. It was the one that Mum and Dad had used back when Daniel and I were born. It had to be there somewhere...

A-ha, eventually I found it – THE BUMPER BOOK OF FOOTBALLER NAMES!

Right, it was time for me to get creative:

J – Did I want something standard like James, or something super cool and important like Jefferson, or Julius, or Jorge? There were so many exciting options!

But just before I chose one, I remembered something. The Tigers would be using my first name a lot. And if they called it out in training, I would need to reply straight away, because that would be my name from now on.

OI, JUPITER?

Silence.

Hmm, maybe it was safer to stick with Johnny after all. Besides, Chris Crawley already knew me. A new look and a new first name would be way too confusing.

N – I probably wouldn't need to use my middle name as Tissbury Tigers Assistant Manager, but I was going undercover, and so it was best to be prepared, just in case. I didn't mind what it was, just as long as it wasn't my real middle name – Nigel. Shhhh, don't tell anyone! Anything was better than that. Neo? Nelson? Neymar?

B – OK, seeing as I couldn't be a Ball any more, I needed something totally brand new and brilliant.

What I wanted was a name that shouted, "I KNOW LOTS ABOUT FOOTBALL, PROMISE!"

So, Johnny...

Balaban?

Beckham?

Bendtner?

Bjørnebye?

Blake?

Boateng?

Bohinen?

Brown?

Bullwinkle?

Butcher?

There were so many to choose from, but which one did I go for? Sorry, you're just going to have to read on to find out!

CHAPTER 4

FIRST-PRACTICE PROBLEMS

"Come on, eat up, darling," Mum said, putting a plate in front of me. "This'll give you extra energy for tonight."

"Thanks, but I'm not hungry."

"Nonsense – you're a growing boy, Johnnykins!" Mum looked shocked, as if I'd just said a really bad word. "Is it the training session – are you feeling nervous?"

Mums already know everything! I gave a very small nod.

"Well, there's no need, Johnny-dumpling. You'll be absolutely wonderful, I just know it! I'm sure the Tigers will be very friendly, and you'll have Daniel there too."

"That's the problem, Mum!"

Don't worry – I didn't actually say that bit. As I said before, I would never tell on Daniel. Instead,

I just thought it really hard until it exploded in my brain. BOOM! Ah, that felt better.

"I know what'll cheer you up." Mum jumped up suddenly. "I was going to wait until later, but I may as well give it to you now..."

Uh-oh.

"...we can always change it if it's not quite the right size, but all the best managers are wearing them..."

Double uh-oh. Whatever my gift was, it was sure to be super embarrassing. Just as long as it wasn't a...

"...a lovely little waistcoat!"

Mum had got this sooooo wrong. I had a problem with each of those three words:

1) It wasn't lovely – in fact, it was as ugly and as scratchy as Grandpa's really old cardigans.

2) It wasn't little – in fact, it was super HUUUUUGE.
And most importantly...

3) IT WAS A WAISTCOAT!

I'll say it loud and clear: I'd rather support Rockley Rangers (URGH!) for the rest of my life than wear a waistcoat in public. But I couldn't say to that to my mum, could I?

"It's … great," I lied, giving her a big, fake family-photo smile. "Thanks … a lot."

My face soon started to ache, and I raced up to my room to hide the waistcoat. I didn't want Daniel to see it – I didn't want ANYONE to see it.

🏆 🏆 🏆

"Johnny, have you got your w—"

"Yes, Mum!" I interrupted just in time.

"What?" Daniel shouted loudly as he lifted his headphones off his ears.

"Nothing. Mum was just asking if I had my w— water bottle."

Quick thinking, Johnny! With a cool-kid nod, my brother put his headphones back on. Phew!

We were on our way to – da da daaaa – MY FIRST TISSBURY TIGERS TRAINING SESSION! and my brain had hit the big red panic button.

Arghhhhhhhhh! CANCEL! ABANDON! ABORT!

I wasn't ready and neither was my new football look. The only hat I'd been able to find was from Dad's fancy-dress wizard outfit (don't ask!), and he didn't have any cowboy boots. So all I had was Grandpa George's scarf, hidden under my biggest coat.

Oh and I WAS wearing the waistcoat. Yes, I know I should have just left it behind, but I also knew that Mum would ask about it. My plan was to take it off and hide it before training started. But then our car, Tiss, got stuck in traffic, making us late.

"See ya later!" Daniel called out, sprinting away from me as soon as the car stopped. "And remember my demandz, yeah?"

How could I forget?! By the time I had caught up with Daniel, all the Tissbury Tigers were already out on the pitch, huddled around their manager.

"Ah here he is!" Chris Crawley called out when he spotted me. Oh well, there was no time for me to ditch the waistcoat now. I would just have to keep my coat on, however hot it got.

Breathe, Johnny, breathe!

"Tigers, I'd like you to meet my new assistant,
Mr Johnny..."

Daniel nudged me with his football superpowers.
Say something, Bro – I mean, Non-bro!

"BULAWAYO!" I blurted out, probably a little
too loudly.

Chris Crawley looked stunned, and Daniel's stare
became a glare. Oh no, maybe my new football
name was a bit too much.

"Err ... actually, just call me Johnny," I spluttered
quickly. "Like, whatever, yeah..."

Boy, being an undercover football genius was going to be waaaay harder than I had expected.

"Johnny here is giving me a helping hand for the rest of the season," Coach Crawley continued. "He's got some great football ideas, so be friendly and listen! Right, Johnny, let me introduce you to the Tigers. This is Temba…"

So this was the super-talented Temba! He was the only other Tiger that I had ever heard my brother talk about. Apparently, he was the team's second-best player (after Daniel himself, of course!).

"Hi!" I said eagerly, but he just nodded back, without saying a word, and with a ball balanced perfectly on his boot. I bet he could have stayed like that for hours, becoming the world's first real footballer statue. Anyway, I opened my brain-book and wrote down – "Temba – not much of a talker".

"…this is Craig…"

I tried again. "Hi!"

This time, I did get a "Hi" back, but he said it with a loud sigh, like when you let the air out of a balloon.

"…this is Connor…"

SILENCE!

"…this is Noah…"

SILENCE!

"…this is Dev…"

YAWN!

No words, just more nods, as Coach Crawley went round the rest of the circle. It was like looking up at the Greek gods that Miss Patel had taught us about at school. The Tigers stood there with their hands on their hips and their strong chins pointing up at the sky, fearless and clearly really good at football. Plus, one guy, Jake, was even growing a BEARD!

CRAIG →   JAKE   CONNOR

NOAH

DEV

TEMBA

"Hi, I'm Jake," he said, smiling down at me like a gentle giant.

So how was I, Johnny Ball: previously an accidental football genius, now undercover, supposed to help these gods to win? It seemed impossible!

"Johnny, I have a special task for you today," Coach said, as the team left for their warm-up. "You don't need to help out with the actual training..."

Phew!

"...I just want you to WATCH. Look out for any weaknesses in our team and try to think of ways to improve them. How does that sound?"

That was it – my special task was to watch? Brilliant! Watching football was something that I could definitely do. I did it every day.

"That sounds great, Chris – I mean Coach!"

"Excellent, let's get started then. Busy week of County Cup celebrations, was it?"

He was looking down at my much bigger than normal belly (the scarf fat-suit, remember?).

"Are you sure you don't want to take that coat off, Johnny? You must be boiling!"

"Err no, I'm fine, thanks."

"OK, but over by that bag of footballs you'll find

something you might want to wear instead."

What?! Back when I became the Tissbury Primary assistant manager, Mr Mann gave me a rubbish whistle. But the Tissbury Tigers was "next level", as Daniel would say, and Coach Crawley had definitely said something to WEAR…

I tried to look super cool as I jogged over, but really my heart was beating really fast. There's only one thing I love more than brand-new football kit:

BRAND-NEW FOOTBALL KIT WITH MY NAME ON IT! Well, my initials anyway, and luckily Coach Crawley didn't know about my middle name, so it just said "JB". It was one of the most beautiful things I had ever seen. This was it now: THE BIG TIME!

"Thanks, Coach – I love it!"

Brilliant, the Tigers jacket would be a much better disguise than a scarf fat-suit, especially with one extra touch…

"Sorry, I was just wondering … do you have a Tigers hat to go with it … please?"

Coach Crawley couldn't say no. "Sure, have mine."

"Wow, thanks!"

And just like that, my new undercover football look was ready.

I know what you're thinking – "You're a football genius, Johnny!" But there was a problem – how was I going to put on my terrific new jacket without everyone seeing my terrible new waistcoat? The Tigers were coming back from their warm-up now, but maybe if I was super fast...

"HA HA HA, WHAT IS THAT, JOHNNY?" Tyler couldn't help himself.

Great, they were pointing and laughing at me already! "Tyler – Team Joker" I scribbled down bitterly in my brain-book as the funny comments kept on coming.

"WHAT A WAISTCOAT WEIRDO!"

"LOOK, HE'S GOT A SADDO SCARF TOO!"

HA HA HA HA HA! Everyone was laughing, everyone except Coach Crawley ... and Daniel. But my big brother wasn't protecting me; oh no, he was just too angry to join in. It was only day one and I had already broken the first two of Daniel's "demandz":

1) Don't wear that saddo scarf.

2) Don't do nothing else embarrassing either.

Oh dear, not a good start. Luckily, Coach Crawley soon blew his whistle for the start of the training drills. So I quickly zipped up my beautiful new Tissbury Tigers jacket and got ready to make some great football notes.

Don't worry – I didn't take out my "JNB" pocket notebook. It was waaaay too soon for Pointing and Laughing: Part 2, so I made notes in my head.

For the next hour, I stood and watched some of the best football I've ever seen up close.

PING! – perfect pass!

BANG! – brilliant shot!

THUMP! – thudding header!

CRUNCH! – crushing tackle!

OLÉ! – outrageous skillz!

For me, it was like landing on a totally different football planet. Woah, what was this new passing and moving thing that I was watching? I had come a very, very long way from those early days of HOOF!ing and hiding at Tissbury Primary, that was for sure. The Tigers players really were gods – Football Gods! No wonder they were near the top of the league.

But who stood out above all the other Tigers like a tower of annoying super talent?

Yes, you guessed it – my big brother, Daniel "The Cannon" Ball.

I'd always thought that Dad was just being Dad

when he boasted that Daniel was "one of the best young players that our town has ever seen". But it turns out, he was right.

Most of the time, Daniel didn't even look like he was trying very hard, but that was because he didn't have to.

The Tigers defenders took it in turns to mark him, trying every tactic, but Daniel was just too smart and skilful for all of them. And he just kept scoring. As much as I hated to admit it right then, my brother really was a future football superstar.

Anyway, enough of that – my brother's head is big enough already. My special assistant manager task was to find weaknesses in the Tigers team.

At first, all I noticed were small things, like:

NUMBER 3 – loves to attack. Tracking back? Not so much.

NUMBER 11 – very left-footed – switch him to right wing so he can cut inside?

But then suddenly, I noticed something much more important. In amongst all those talented Tigers, there was an odd one out.

CHAPTER 5

ODD ONE OUT

OK, you can play right-back, Johnny. Right back in the changing rooms – ha ha ha ha ha!

Yes, thanks to Billy Newland, the biggest bully at Tissbury Primary, I knew that right-back was the number one worst position on the whole football pitch. Well, other than left-back maybe...

Left back on the team bus – ha ha ha ha ha!

I also knew that right-back was where you normally put a player who ~~sucked~~ wasn't so good. And boy was the Tissbury Tigers Number 2 one of

those players. In a team full of fantasy footballers, he stood out like a beaver at a barbecue, and not in a good way.

- He was the tallest player in the team, and the thinnest too. He was like a walking lamp-post!
- He played with his head down, as if he was always ready for someone to say something mean about him, even though no one ever did.
- He had matchstick legs that looked like they might snap at any moment. Argh! In striped socks, they reminded me of the rulers we used in Maths class.
- And when he ran, it was like he was moving in super-slow motion, springing from foot to foot. With his arms flailing, he looked like he was always trying to escape from something (or someone).

"Poor guy," I thought to myself. After all, I certainly knew how it felt to be the odd one out on a football field. The game was going on around him, as if he was just one of Coach Crawley's marker cones. No one wanted to pass to Number 2 and when he did get the ball, no one got it back. EVERYTHING went wrong:

When he tried to HOOF! it downfield, he ended up smashing the ball all the way onto the changing room roof.

Sorry!

When he tried to play a super-simple sideways pass, he kicked the ball so hard that it crashed off his teammate's foot and went straight to the opposition striker.

Sorry!

When he tried to take a throw-in, the ball ended up landing at his own feet.

Sorry!

And with each mistake, his shoulders slumped lower and lower until he looked like he might topple face-first down into the mud.

As I've said already, "Poor guy." He was so far out of his depth that he didn't even bother calling out, "Help!" The Football Gods just ignored him and got on with the game.

But why was this Number 2 playing for a top team like the Tissbury Tigers? That's what I needed to find out. If they were serious about winning the league, surely they should find someone better?

"Psssst … Daniel!" I shout-whispered at the end of training.

We were walking back to the car. Not together, though. Oh no, we couldn't be seen together. I had to be an undercover football genius, remember? So my brother was staying ten steps ahead of me, as if he had no idea who I was.

"Come on, no one's even looking!" I told him. "Anyway, you could just say that you were giving me a lift home because I live nearby."

("Actually, I live in the bedroom next to yours!" I thought, but managed not to say. I was getting a lot better at that.)

It didn't work, though. Daniel still wouldn't say a word to me until we were safely in the car. Then, "What's up, Bro?" he said with a smile as he nodded at Dad, as if the last hour had all been a dream (or rather NIGHTMARE). Unbelievable!

"That Number 2 – what's the deal with him? Is he always that bad?"

Daniel nodded and then did his cool-kid shrug. "Pretty much, yeah. Craig's proper flushed at football."

That was it?! My brother usually got angry if Mum even tried to say, "Did you sleep well?" to him at breakfast, so why was he being so calm about a player who might stop his team from winning the league title for the first time in years? It didn't make sense.

"So why is he in the team then?"

"Because he's Craig Crawley..."

I know that people sometimes call me a football genius, but my brain doesn't always "play Ball" (ha ha, geddit?). Plus, Daniel has ZERO patience these days.

"...duh, he's the manager's son!"

Yeah, duuuuuh, Johnny! Why hadn't I thought of that? And then I got one of those super-awful sinking feelings, all the way down to the bottom of my stomach...

Uh-oh, what had I done?! At the end of the training session, I had scribbled a few notes in my pocket notebook (when no one was looking, obviously) – "WAYS TO MAKE THE TISSBURY TIGERS

(EVEN) BETTER". And I had given the list to Coach Crawley before I left! On that piece of paper, there were ten ideas and six of them were about the same player. Yep, you guessed it – Craig Crawley, HIS SON:

✍ JNB

NUMBER 2 – needs to play with his head up
NUMBER 2 – needs to work on his strength
NUMBER 2 – needs to work on his speed
NUMBER 2 – needs to work on his passing
NUMBER 2 – needs to work on his throw-ins
NUMBER 2 – needs to work on his tackling

I was in biiig trouble, and on my very first day in the job. At least I hadn't written down my last, really mean thought, though:

Number 2 – needs to be dropped from the team.

But still, Coach Crawley wouldn't be happy with me. What was I going to do – go on another scary adventure with Tabia to get the notes back?

No, I had a better (and safer) idea. I knew a really old man who could help.

CHAPTER 6

GREAT ADVICE FROM GRANDPA GEORGE

"AH, IF IT ISN'T THE TIDDLYTASTIC NEW TISSBURY TIGERS ASSISTANT MANAGER!" Grandpa George shouted loudly as he wrapped me in his really, really long arms as we stood on the doorstep.

Either Grandpa George was super proud of me and wanted to let the whole street know about my success, or he hadn't turned his new hearing aid on yet.

"WHAT DID YOU SAY, WHIPPER-SNAPPER?"

I hadn't said anything.

"ONE SECOND, SONNY JIM," he yelled out, slamming the front door behind us.

Sonny Jim? My name is Johnny! But there's no point correcting Grandpa George. You'll learn: he has his own weird and wonderful (and really old) words for everything. Mum says that one day she's going to put them all in a special Grandpa dictionary.

Anyway, Grandpa George stood there fiddling with his right ear for ages until finally his face froze in a great big grin. **_TING! LIGHT-BULB MOMENT._** I make the same face when I get one of my great football ideas.

"Well, that's ballooning better, isn't it!" he said, a lot less loudly this time. "Now, will you have some tea, miladdy?"

"Yes, please, Grandpa George!"

Once we were sitting down with our drinks, Grandpa George leaned back in his chair and put the really, really long fingers of his two really, really long hands together. When he did that, it meant he was ready for a "jibber-jabber", or a "chat" as the rest of us like to call it.

"So, what can I do for my favourite little follyflop?"

Grandpa George used to be an assistant manager too, back when he was waaaay, waaaay younger, so I was hoping that he could help me. He knew lots about football, and as I told the story of my first training session and the not-very-good Number 2, he kept nodding his head like one of those toy dogs some people have in their cars.

Was he falling asleep, right when I needed his help? No, like most really old people, Grandpa George had just heard it all before.

"Ho ho ho, football never chuffing changes, does it? My old manager, Malcolm McCleary – he had a son too ... yes, Maxwell. Absolute codswallop he was – he could hardly kick the hallouming ball! But for years, his name was still there on the team sheet, every winking week."

"Was he a right-back too?"

"No, he was a right twit, actually! He really was one of the worst wasters-of-spacers to ever walk the football field."

"So, how did you get him out of the team, Grandpa George?"

"I didn't, ducky. Luckily Maxwell met a luverly lady and they moved to Mozambique."

Well, that didn't help ME, did it! Craig Crawley was only thirteen – he still had at least (trying to do the Maths, trying to do the Maths...), whatever, LOTS of years of being a rubbish right-back before he was even old enough to fall in love and leave Tissbury.

Grandpa George must have seen the "No, I need a better idea than that!" look on my face, because he started doing a lot of "Hmm"ing.

"Do you remember that blinking ball grog you had in your County Cup team?" he asked at last.

Grandpa George was talking about Izzy and he meant ball hog, not grog, but I nodded anyway.

"Well, how did you solve that stinkbomb?"

"I organized a group dance-off to show her that the team had to work together if we wanted to win."

"Exact-atootly! TIDDLYTASTIC new Tissbury Tigers Assistant Manager, it's your job to make the team work together, and to help that waster-of-spacer to waste less space!"

Everything always sounded so easy (and exciting) when Grandpa George said it, sitting in his comfy chair with a cup of tea.

But really, trying to turn Craig Crawley into a fairly good footballer ... while at the same time making sure that the Tissbury Tigers became a title-winning team ... while at the same time staying undercover ... was going to be my toughest task yet. I would have to be a real football genius – or a wizard, maybe – to pull that hat-trick off. And there was still one more problem...

"Thanks, Grandpa George, but what about Coach Crawley? Should I say sorry for writing all those mean things about his son?"

This time, there was no need for any "Hmm"ing.

"Well, if you can coach his son to kick the kiccupping ball, then he'll love you for ever, won't he?!"

As always, Grandpa George was right. If I did that, Coach Crawley might even promote me to, I dunno, "NEARLY BUT NOT QUITE MANAGER"!

But no, I was getting ahead of myself. I hadn't said more than "Hi!" to Craig, or to any of the other Tigers. To them, I was still just a little "waistcoat weirdo" who thought he knew a lot about football and definitely was NOT Daniel "The Cannon" Ball's brother.

"You know what I'm going to say next, don't you, grasshopper?" Grandpa George added after a last long slurp of tea.

Yes, I did – I had "wallops of work" to do.

CHAPTER 7

ATTACK OF THE FLYING FULL-BACK

TISSBURY TIGERS VS WESTON WARTHOGS

"Not so fast, my Tissbury treasures!" Mum said to us when we arrived at the football ground. She was just in time because Daniel was already halfway out the car door. "Now, boys, it's your first Tigers game together, so could I please have just one nice photo of the two of you?"

She had her phone in her hand, but knowing Mum, it would still take her aaaages and all she'd end up with would be a super-blurry shot. Trust me, I've been alive for a lot of Christmases now.

For once, Daniel and I could agree on something – "No way, Mum!"

"Oh, darling dearests, pleeeeaaaase!"

Then Dad tried playing the not-quite-so-embarrassing parent. "Come on lads, your mother is asking you very nicely. Just one quick SNAP! Hey, don't make me come after you … owwwww, my ankle!" Ah Dad's famous ankle injury – his excuse for everything!

My brother was gone, swaggering off with his headphones in, just like the pros. And I was right behind him – well, ten steps behind him, just to make sure that no one spotted us together. But really, I was miles away, searching my brain for some great last-minute football ideas.

Think, Johnny, think!

I had my "head in the cows" as Grandpa George would say, and that's why I didn't really think about this next bit until much later on. Between the car park and the changing room, there's this wild bit of green, which is mostly just brambles and stingy nettles. "The Bush of Lost Balls", the Tigers call it. Anyway, as I walked past, I saw something out of the corner of my left eye, lurking in the shadows. Weird, huh? It was tall and thin like a walking lamp-post, but remember, my mind was on the match.

Think, Johnny, think!

It was a real crunch game for the Tigers – they all were now. We (yes, we – I was part of the team too!) were still two points behind the league leaders, the

Cooperston Cobras, and today we were taking on the Weston Warthogs, who were only two points behind us in third place. In case all that talk of twos was super confusing, basically the top of the table looked like this:

Position	Team	Played	Won	Drawn	Lost	Total
1	Cooperston Cobras	12	10	1	1	31
2	Tissbury Tigers	12	9	2	1	29
3	Weston Warthogs	12	8	3	1	27

So this match was a must-win for the Tigers, and who knew, maybe they would need an undercover football genius to help save the—

"Merry Match Day, Johnny!" Coach Crawley called out cheerfully as I entered the team changing room.

"Merry Match Day, Coach!" I called back.

Phew, it was like my "WAYS TO MAKE THE TISSBURY TIGERS (EVEN) BETTER" list had never happened.

But Coach Crawley had 121 per cent read my notes because when he called out the team, Number 11 (Reggie, in case you were wondering) was starting on the right wing, instead of the left, just like I had suggested. That was the good news.

The not-so-good news? The not-so-good Number 2 was still right there at right-back.

Never mind, it was time for Part One of my new assistant manager master plan: PRE-MATCH CHAT WITH CRAIG.

I waited until he was warming up on his own near the corner flag, and then walked over, pulling my Tigers hat down low and looking as cool-kid casual as I could.

"Hi … m–mate–y," I said, as if I had never spoken to a human before in my life. "F–feeling …pumped for the … game?"

What a disaster! Oh boy, I really had to learn how to talk to teenagers.

Anyway, after that first sigh of a "Hi!" and then watching him play football (badly), I was expecting Craig to be nervous, or shy, or a bit dopey. But no, despite being Coach Crawley's son, he was just plain mean. He screwed his eyes up at me and hissed like a horrible snake:

"I'm not your 'mate–y', you waistcoat weirdo!"

"Hey, I'm not wearing that any more. My mum made me w—"

Suddenly, an evil smirk spread across Craig's

face, like he had just discovered my deepest, darkest secret. "Whatevs, no one wants you here, so why don't you take your saddo scarf and your fake football ideas and run back to Mummy, yeah? That's where a kid like you belongs!" Woah, it turned out that Craig wasn't nice AT ALL. I didn't feel one tiny bit sorry for him any more – he deserved to be "flushed" at football. I made a quick note to myself: "be careful around Craig Crawley!"

Part One of my new assistant manager master plan had been a "flopping great" failure, as Grandpa George would say. But now our must-win match was about to kick off!

"GO, DANNY DEAREST!"

"LOVE YOU, JOHNNY-BUNNY!"

It was really hard to be an undercover football genius when my super-embarrassing mum was there watching and cheering for BOTH of her sons. But with my hand-shield up, I just about managed to focus...

If I liked the silly things that football people come out with, I would say that the first half was "a tense stalemate". But I don't, so I'll just say: "pretty boring". It was still a whole lot better than watching Tissbury Primary (sorry, guys!), but we want to see goals, don't we? And it was 0–0.

The Tigers midfield had the ball most of the time, but Aroon and Finn (don't worry, I'll give you the full team sheet soon!) could only move it from side to side, like scuttling crabs on a beach. There was no way through because the Weston Warthogs hadn't come to Tissbury to play football. They had come to "park the bus". All of their players were inside their own half, and three of them were marking Daniel so tightly that he could probably smell their bad defender breath.

"Come on, Tissbury!" Coach Crawley clapped encouragingly. "Find that killer pass!"

OK, I'll admit it – my idea to switch Reggie to the right wing really wasn't working. The Weston left-back knew exactly what he was going to do every time – cut inside onto his "lush" left foot and cross it. It was like playing against a rubbish robot, waaaay too easy. And Dev was having the same problems on the other wing. His silky skillz weren't getting him anywhere.

"Any more ideas, Johnny?" Coach Crawley asked at half-time. I know it was early days, but I couldn't help noticing that he didn't do a lot of thinking for himself.

At least it was giving me the chance to show the Tigers that I wasn't just a primary school waistcoat weirdo. I was the future number one football genius in the whole wide world, and I was here to help.

Think, Johnny, think!

"Not yet, Coach," I replied, "I'm working on it!"

I needed to find a way through the strong wall of Warthog defenders. A 0–0 draw wasn't an option.

As the second half went on, I could see that Daniel was getting more and more frustrated up front. He wasn't used to not winning, OR not scoring. At one point, he got so angry that he even glared over at ME. I'm not an expert on cool-kid looks, but I'm pretty sure it meant:

Please, undercover football genius – help me save the day!

Or something like that anyway. I knew that all my super-talented big brother needed was one half-chance to be the hero...

TING! LIGHT-BULB MOMENT. At last, another idea. Sorry, I know it's bad to boast, but boy was it a great one! I raced over to Coach Crawley and quickly whispered my idea. He seemed a bit surprised that I hadn't just said it out loud, but if you've got a really clever plan, you should always whisper it, just in case. Especially when you're undercover.

"Great, let's give it a go!"

The next time the ball went out for a Tigers throw-in, I whispered the plan to our left-back, Connor, who then raced up the wing to whisper it to Dev.

Ready?

Ready!

Right, it was time for...

ATTACK OF THE FLYING FULL-BACK!

Why did I decide to do it on the left? Yep, you guessed it – because Craig was on the right! It doesn't take a football genius to work out that our Number 2 wasn't going to get us a winning goal.

Our Number 3, on the other hand... I only knew three things about Connor so far: 1) he was left-footed, 2) he was super speedy and 3) he loved to attack. But that was enough – he was perfect for my plan! The next time Dev got the ball and cut inside onto his right foot...

ZOOM! Connor burst forward on the outside, down the left wing, like he was running the next leg of an Olympic relay race.

See? Attack of the Flying Full-back! The Warthog defenders just stood there watching, not knowing what to do, as...

"Yes!" Connor called out for the ball and, with a fancy back-heel, Dev passed it through to him. Now, he just needed to cross it into the box...

Watching from the sidelines, the next bit was like a slow-motion movie scene (and thankfully Craig wasn't the one moving in slow-mo this time). The ball seemed to float through the air for aaaages, and so did my superstriker brother. **THUMP!**

GOOOOOOOOOOOOOAAAAAAAAAAALLLLLLLLLL!

We had done it! I had done it! I had won the game for the Tigers with a moment of genuine football genius. What a start! I couldn't help punching the air with both fists, but I did stop myself from doing the running knee slide. It was too soon for that. That could wait until we won the league title.

As the players jogged back to the halfway line, Daniel gave me a little cool-kid nod that I think meant, *Thanks so much, Bro. You really are a football genius!*

But best of all, Connor gave me a cool-kid fist

bump (always one knuckle, NEVER two) and then said a whole twelve words to me: "Johnny, that was a well sick football idea. Welcome to the Tigers!"

MATCH REPORT 1   🖐 JNB

TISSBURY TIGERS 1–0 WESTON WARTHOGS

STARTING LINE-UP (MARKS OUT OF 10):
Noah 6, Craig 2, Connor 8, Beardy Jake 6,
Tyler 6, Finn 6, Aroon 5, Dev 7, Daniel 7,
Temba 6, Reggie 6

SCORER:
Daniel, of course!

WHAT WENT WELL:
1) We won – thanks to me! (and Daniel, I guess)
2) Craig Crawley didn't have anything to do
   (badly)

EVEN BETTER IF:
1) Craig wasn't a) so nasty and b) so flushed
   at football
2) Our midfield sometimes passed the ball
   FORWARD instead of sideways all the time

CHAPTER 8

COACH CRAWLEY'S SECOND SPECIAL TASK

"Come here, my two little Tissbury triumphs!"
Mum squealed, squeezing us waaaay too tightly.
Whether we liked it or not (NOT!), Daniel and I were
now the slices of bread in a proud-Mum sandwich.

Don't worry, we were back home by then, so the Tigers would never find out about that super-embarrassing situation. Operation: Undercover Football Genius was still under control.

As soon as I could escape, I raced around the corner to share the news with Grandpa George.

"HO HO HO, WHAT AN INCREDI-BALL IDEA, JOHNNY!"

This time, his hearing aid was definitely on; he was just super proud of us.

"The football world had better watch out for you Barnstorming Ball Brothers!"

"That's right, Grandpa George!" I roared, with my hands on my hips like a superhero.

"The Barnstorming Ball Brothers" – yes, suddenly I could see us on *Match of the Day* together, with our faces in every newspaper. Because after we won the league title, I wouldn't need to be an undercover football genius any more...

🏆 🏆 🏆

There was still one last person that I couldn't wait to tell about the "Attack of the Flying Full-back!"

"Nice one, *HEXAGON-HEAD!*" Tabia cheered

when I finished my story on the walk to school on Monday morning.

Maths was her new favourite subject, and now she was even using it to beat me in our nasty name battles. It was so unfair! She knew that I couldn't compete, not yet anyway.

"Thanks … **DIVISION-DINGO?**"

What? It was the best that I could come up with early on a Monday morning! Tabia, on the other hand, always had smart things to throw at me.

"You're welcome, **FRACTION-FREAK!** I miss you being the Tissbury Primary manager, though. We really suck without your great football ideas. You're a bazillion times better than Mr Mann!"

I was pretty sure that wasn't a real number, but I kept that thought to myself because my best friend was just trying to be nice and plus, she already looked really fed up.

"You don't need me, Tabs," I lied. "With you in the team, Tissbury Primary could win against anyone."

(That second part is true; she's got mad football skillz. If you don't believe me, just ask anyone at our school.)

Thankfully, Tabia looked a tiny bit happier after

that. "Fine, stay with your stupid Tigers then!" she groaned dramatically, rolling her eyes just like her mum. "So, go on – what did Coach Crawley say to you after the game?"

I put on my best "I'm a really friendly football manager" voice:

"Well done, Johnny – you're off to a flying start! Let's meet before training on Wednesday to talk about your next special task."

"Ooooo, what do you think it'll be?" Tabia said with wide, excited eyes. Her imagination was off, zipping around like a bee on a bouncy castle.

"Maybe he'll ask you to go and spy on the Rockley Raptors..."

"I hope not – I'm already working undercover!"

"Or maybe he'll ask you to take over the Tigers because he's got to go to prison ... or on holiday to Hawaii..."

"What? What planet are you on?"

"Earth ... I think."

🏆 🏆 🏆

As you've probably guessed, when I spoke to him before our next training session, Coach Crawley's second special task for me turned out to be waaaay less weird than any of Tabia's ideas. And, of course, it involved the Tigers' not-so-good Number 2.

"So, I read your notes, Johnny," Coach Crawley told me in his "office", which was actually just the store cupboard where we kept the balls and cones. "I agree with all your ideas, and that's why I think you're the perfect man – I mean boy – for this job."

"What job is that, Coach?"

"Johnny, I want you to do some extra training with Craig, to work on those issues that you picked out in your notes. Obviously, I would love to do it myself,

but I've got the whole team to coach, haven't I?
So, what do you think?"

What I was really thinking:

ME, WORKING ONE-ON-ONE WITH THAT
WORM EVERY WEEK? NO, THANKS!

vs what I said I was thinking:

SURE, COACH - ANYTHING I CAN DO TO HELP THE TIGERS.

"That's brilliant. Thanks, JB – I knew I could count
on you!"

Oh boy, where was I even going to start? I
decided I would begin with what I thought was the
easiest of the six "issues":

Number 2 – needs to work on his throw-ins.

I mean, everyone can chuck a ball, right? So I
grabbed a big bag of them and walked over to
Craig, who was on his own near the corner flag
again. On the way, I tried my best to think positively:

Maybe he was just having a really bad day the
last time I talked to him.

He's Coach Crawley's son – he can't be that cruel!

Surely this second meeting can't go as badly as
the first one – can it?

"Hi, I-I'm here to practise some throw-ins with you."

I was wrong; our second meeting was worse. This time, Craig just laughed in my face. "Why would I want to do that, you waistcoat weirdo?"

OK, it was official – he totally hated my guts. Sorry, there was no way that I could complete Coach Crawley's second special task. His son was just a) too nasty and b) too flushed at football. THE END.

But wait, no, I couldn't give up already, not without at least a bit of a fight. I wanted to prove that I would do anything to help the Tigers. So I tried again:

"I don't really want to do this either, but your dad – I mean, Coach Crawley – he asked me to."

"Yeah, well he can't make me do ANYTHING! And neither can you, Johnny B... What was your stupid surname again?"

Craig had a look on his face, like a detective who's just smelled a fart. Uh-oh, which new football name had I gone for in the end?

Think, Johnny, think!

"B–Bulawayo," I remembered, just in time. Not that Craig seemed to care any more.

"Whatevs, waistcoat weirdo." He shrugged.

One thing was for sure: it was definitely time for him to get a new insult.

OK, try number three: "Look, we don't need to talk to each other, OK? You can just throw these five balls as far as you can, and then I'll go get them. How about that?"

When Craig picked up the first ball, I stupidly thought my plan had worked and he was going to do what I said. But no, he had a different idea.

GO GET THAT BALL! he yelled.

It wasn't a throw-in; it was a lob-at. A lob at me. A lob right in my ... gut.

THUD!

OWWWWWW!

I was shocked for three reasons:

1) I was winded, so I could barely breathe.

2) For someone who couldn't take a throw-in, he could really hurl a ball hard!

And...

3) Wait a second, what had he just said? "Go get that BALL!"

Uh-oh, did Craig somehow know that I was secretly Daniel's brother? But I had been so careful about staying undercover! Had our football-boot black hair given it away, despite my hat? Was it my super-long scarf? Was it our super-embarrassing mum?

OR maybe Craig had been spying on me all along! Because that's when I remembered that tall, thin object I had spotted, lurking in the bushes before the Warthogs match. Could that walking lamp-post have been him?

OR was Craig just talking about the actual football he had just lobbed at me? It was really hard to tell, but he was starting to sound a lot like...

CLANK ... CLANK ... CLANK!

"Oh, I nearly forgot!" Craig smirked like a really vile villain. "I invited someone along to train with us tonight. I think you might know him – from PRIMARY SCHOOL!"

CHAPTER 9

BILLY'S BACK!

Noooooo, Billy was back!

"All right, Johnny?" he bellowed. I could already see the big, ugly grin on his big, ugly face. "I bet you're pleased to see me. I've come to PLAY BALL!"

If you haven't met Billy Newland before, my advice is – don't bother. He goes to my school and he's the biggest bully I had ever met ... well, until Craig Crawley came along, of course. And now the two of them had teamed up together to try to ruin my undercover football coaching career. It was my worst nightmare!

But how did they know each other? Maybe Billy had started a "We Hate Johnny Ball" after-school club behind my back.

Anyway, I had to find a way to stop the terrible twosome telling the Tigers who I really was. Otherwise, Daniel was going to 1) kick me off the team, and then 2) probably kill me.

Think, Johnny, think!

I was hoping that when Coach Crawley saw Billy, he would tell him that training was for team members only. That's what most managers would do, right? But no, Coach was so chilled out that he could have survived in a freezer for months.

"Welcome, the more the merrier I always say!"

Why, oh why, did he have to be so ... friendly?! OK, I needed a proper plan, and quickly. But now that Billy had BOSH!ed his way in and started talking to the rest of the team, Craig had changed his mind about throw-ins. Suddenly, they were his favourite thing to do in the whole world.

"MORE! MORE! MORE!" he kept yelling at me, like a kid on a swing.

The worst part was that Craig's evil plan was working. I was getting more and more frustrated. Meanwhile, Billy was over there, HOOF!ing and GOOF!ing with the Tigers on the pitch.

What was he saying to them? Was he talking about me? Was he talking about Daniel?

I should have been there, making sure that Billy didn't blow my cover, but instead I was stuck helping horrible Craig learn how to chuck a ballooning ball. Sometimes being an assistant manager really SUCKS!

"OK, that's enough," I said eventually. "Let's go join the others."

We got there during a drinks break. Billy looked like he was having the best time ever, and so did his new audience.

"Oh hi, Johnny," he bellowed out at me. "I was just telling the guys about that absolute BANGER I scored to win the County Cup. Remember? Oh yeah, sorry, you were on the pitch too, weren't you? I forgot because you were normally just the BALL BOY!"

Billy was really on a roll now, like a skunk on a scooter. Well, that had to stop. I needed to shut his big bully mouth before he started talking about my brother. But how?

Think, Johnny, think!

TING! LIGHT-BULB MOMENT.

I raced back to the changing

room and grabbed Daniel's phone from his coat pocket (according to Mum and Dad, I was still too young to have my own, but that's an argument for another day...). Luckily, I had worked out my brother's secret password (shhhh, don't tell him!), and once I was close enough for Coach Crawley to hear, I played a random ringtone:

DIDDLY, DIDDLY, DIDDLY, DEEEE!

Right, it was time for me to become – da da daaa – Johnny Ball: Undercover ACTOR Genius...

"Hello? Oh, hi there ... David," I said, going for my best "important football person" name.

PHONE PAUSE!

Coach was looking over at me, so I copied Mum's "One second, sorry I'm just on a call" hand gesture. I was putting on a strong performance so far.

"Really?" I asked no one loudly. "Rockley Raptors have sent a spy to come and watch the Tissbury Tigers train? Are you sure?"

PHONE PAUSE!

Yep, Coach was still 121 per cent listening.

"Right, well thanks for letting us know, David. What does the spy look like?"

PHONE PAUSE!

"Year 5 ... wearing the latest Tissbury Town kit ... and gold boots? Interesting... Thanks again, David. Say hi to ... Sue and the ... girls. Bye."

I know, I know, I could be a movie star, couldn't I, if I didn't love football so much? I moved "famous actor" up to Career Plan B, and "international ice-cream taster" down to C.

"Everything OK, JB?" Coach Crawley asked when I walked back over.

"Hmm not really, Coach. That was David ... Matthews, one of my football friends. Apparently, the Rockley Raptors have sent a spy to watch our training session. Can you believe it? A boy with gold boots..."

Coach Crawley looked over at Billy, and then down at his sparkling feet. Gotcha! With a sigh, he said, "I suppose we'd better ask him to leave then."

I tried to look sad too, but it was tricky. "I agree, Coach. It's a shame, but we have NO choice."

Surprise, surprise – Billy wasn't very happy about being booted out.

"Hey, get your hands off me! I'm not going anywhere – I play for the Tigers now. Tell them, Craig!"

"I'm sorry, kiddo," Coach told him calmly, "but we can't take any risks right now..."

"You won't get away with this, Johnny B—"

"Be quiet, Billy!" Phew! I stopped him just in time. "We all know that you're a Rockley Raptors spy."

"No, I'm not! What are you talking about? Prove it – I bet you can't! Whatever, the Tigers are trash anyway..."

At last, Billy's angry bellowing stopped, and the Tigers could practise in peace again! I had won this time, but my struggles as an undercover football genius were far from over.

CHAPTER 10

YOU SNOOZE, YOU LOSE

TISSBURY TIGERS VS MAYBRIDGE MAGPIES

"Why the foot-long face, Bro? Maybridge are well mid-table. Last year, we smashed 'em 12–0, so you can probs play it cool today."

"OK!" I replied, nearly choking on my Three-a-Fried breakfast. It was still pretty early on a Saturday morning and Daniel had just said ACTUAL WORDS to me. Or was it a spooky brother-ghost speaking? It was nearly as shocking as the time Dad tried to do "The Worm" at a family wedding.

But that's another story for another day – back to the Tigers. Surely Daniel's morning miracle was a good sign, right? Maybe I didn't need to feel so nervous about being an assistant manager, for once. To make sure, I quickly checked the league table:

Position	Team	Played	Won	Drawn	Lost	Total
1	Cooperston Cobras	13	11	1	1	34
2	Tissbury Tigers	13	10	2	1	32
6	Maybridge Magpies	13	6	2	5	20

Daniel was right; the Magpies were well mid-table! Their record so far was:

WIN, LOSS, WIN, LOSS, DRAW

WIN, LOSS, WIN, LOSS, DRAW

WIN, LOSS, WIN...

LOSS! I could feel confidence spreading over me like peanut butter on toast. The Tigers were going to eat the Magpies alive, and I could just sit back and enjoy a...

"Merry Match Day, JB!"

"Merry Match Day, Coach!"

As the Tigers warmed up, everyone seemed super psyched about the game. Everyone except Craig, of course. He looked as miserable as ever, all alone near the corner flag.

"What are YOU looking at, waistcoat weirdo?"

Nope, I still didn't feel sorry for him.

There were no surprises on Coach Crawley's team sheet this time. Reggie was back on the left again, with Dev on the right.

FWEEEEET! KICK-OFF!

"UP AND AT 'EM, DANNY-DIDDLE!"

"SHOW 'EM WHO'S COACH, JOHNNY-PICKLE!"

Even Dad was finding Mum super embarrassing. He had moved waaaay down the touchline, "to get a better view of Daniel," he said,

GOAL!

GOAL!

GOAL!

Before I could even put my hand-shield up, we were winning 3–0. Daniel had already scored two goals and he was on the hunt for another hat-trick to add to his record.

"Well, I guess I won't be needing this today," I thought, putting my pocket notebook away.

Wow, was it game over already? That's what the Tigers thought. Suddenly, Beardy Jake was trying to dribble out of defence, and our sideways-pass midfielders were trying to showboat like superstars.

That was a big mistake, though, because the Magpies were well mid-table, remember? So after ten minutes of terrible football, they suddenly woke up and played ten minutes of terrific football.

Beardy Jake lost the ball on the edge of our box and **BANG!** 3–1!

The showboaters rainbow-flicked it straight to the Magpies striker – 3–2!

"FOCUS!" Coach Crawley called out. He was as angry as a really friendly football manager can get.

But it was no use. The Magpies winger flew past slow-mo Craig and crossed it for … 3–3!

"Why are you SO FLUSHED?" Daniel stormed, turning a full 360 to glare at every single teammate. "All of you!"

Wow, I had only ever seen my brother get that angry at ME before. The sleeping Tigers were in big trouble now. We got to half-time without letting in any more goals, but what the players needed was an almighty TEAM-TALK TELLING-OFF. Stuff like:

Do you call that defending? I call that a DISGRACE!

You boys aren't fit to wear the Tigers stripes!

If you don't start playing properly again soon, you can wave that league title goodbye!

But Coach Crawley wasn't that kind of coach.

"I don't know what to say," he began, which is something that even I know a football manager should never ever start with. "I'm very … DISAPPOINTED."

Was that it? "Disappointed"? That word never works EVER, and especially not on moody teenagers. If you don't believe me, just ask Mum!

For the next few minutes, the Tigers sat there sucking on their half-time oranges and glaring at each other – Daniel at Beardy Jake, Beardy Jake at

Aroon, Aroon at Finn, Finn at Craig, Craig at me (of course)... No, no, no! The players were just passing the blame around like it was a game of pass the parcel. They needed to "take a long, hard look at themselves", as our scary headmaster likes to say, and then find their football passion again; they needed a...

TING! LIGHT-BULB MOMENT. Maybe what the Tigers needed was an ASSISTANT MANAGER'S MOTIVATIONAL TALK ... from me!

No more playground pranks and no more playing it cool - this was my big chance to step up and show my new team that I was a proper football coach. With my chest puffed out like a proud pigeon, I stepped into the Tigers circle and cleared my throat...

But no, I wasn't quite brave enough to make one big team speech yet, so instead I made lots of little ones:

Deep breath... "Beardy Jake, no more messing around – OK? Stick to what you're so good at – winning headers and being big and strong."

Deep breath… "Aroon and Finn, those fancy flicks have got to stop. You're waaaay better than that. From now on, pass the ball like proper midfielders – on the floor and FORWARD!"

Super-deep breath… "Err … keep going, Craig."

Double-super-deep breath… "Bro— I mean Daniel, you're flaming it out there, of course. But I was just thinking – instead of just getting really angry up front, maybe you could shout something a bit more, err, helpful? You know, to support your teammates. I-it's just an idea…"

I made sure that I moved away quickly before he had time to say anything back. I just hoped that I hadn't broken another one of Daniel's "demandz":

5) Don't EVER try to coach ME.

Oh well, by the time the second half started, I was ready for a sit-down, or even a nap. Boy, talking can be really tiring sometimes! So, would Johnny Ball: Assistant Manager Motivator make any difference?

At first, the answer was "not really". Daniel just sulked around being silent-angry, Beardy Jake went back to being big and strong, and the Tigers midfield went back to being really boring on the ball, but they still didn't look like a winning team,

Pass to the left, pass to the right, pass to the left, pass to the right, backwards!

Luckily for ~~Craig~~ us, the Magpies attack had gone back to looking "well mid-table" again too. But at this rate, the only way we were going to score a winning goal was if our deadly dull passing sent our opponents to sleep.

TING! LIGHT-BULB MOMENT.

Spoiler alert: No, we didn't turn them into zombie Magpies – I told you, no more playground pranks! But we did catch them napping at the back...

This time, I didn't even bother whispering my plan to Coach Crawley. I already knew what he would say: "Great, let's give it a go!"

So instead, I just got out my pocket notebook again and wrote the plan down on a fresh new page. Then I passed it to Reggie, who passed it across to Finn, who passed it across to Aroon, who passed it across to Dev. I know: BORING, right? But it was all leading up to another great football idea, I promise...

Reggie: cool-kid nod.

Finn: cool-kid nod.

Aroon: cool-kid nod.

Dev: cool-kid nod ... or just woken up (not sure which).

Right, we were ready to play what I like to call ... PASS, PASS, PASS, PASS, PASS, PASS, PASS, PASS ... FORWARD PASS, SHOOT!

(Hmm, I think I'll have to work on that name.)

Reggie started the move on the left, with a simple sideways pass to Finn. YAWN!

Then Finn played a simple sideways pass to Aroon. YAWN!

Aroon passed to Dev. YAWN!

Dev passed it back to Aroon. YAWN!

And then Aroon passed it back to Finn. YAWN!

As that ball moved boringly on and on and on, back and forth across the pitch, I could see the Magpies defenders' eyelids starting to droop (and dozy Dev's too)...

Hey you, wake up – here's where it gets good, I promise! Because when Aroon got the ball again, you were probably expecting him to play another simple sideways pass to Dev on the right. YAWN! Well, that's what the Maybridge defenders were expecting anyway, but this time Aroon played a fantastic long FORWARD pass through to Daniel. *PING!* Perfect!

At first, my brother was as shocked as the Magpies. A forward pass? To him? In the penalty area? But luckily, he soon snapped out of it and *BANG! GOAL!*

Daniel had a hat-trick and it was now 4–3 to the Tigers! My plan had worked perfectly, so perfectly that I would have waved my super-long scarf above my head like a cowboy lasso if it hadn't been hidden under my jacket. So instead, I just punched the air softly and played it sort of cool.

"Yes, Johnny!"

"Tidy tactics, J!

"You've got football FLAIR, lil man!"

That was Reggie, Finn and Aroon, giving me cool-kid compliments and cool-kid high fives too (always one hand, NEVER two).

Daniel was off superstriker-celebrating on his own, but I was feeling so proud of myself that I didn't care about that. Hopefully, if my great football ideas kept working so well, one day my brother would be proud of me too.

There was even enough time for Beardy Jake to score another one by just being big and strong.

THUD! GOAL!

5–3 – phew! Thanks to me and my (undercover) football genius, the Tigers were still in the title race.

MATCH REPORT 2   🖐 JNB

TISSBURY TIGERS 5-3 MAYBRIDGE MAGPIES

STARTING LINE-UP (MARKS OUT OF 10):
Noah 6, Craig 2, Connor 6, Beardy Jake 7,
Tyler 6, Finn 7, Aroon 8, Dev 7, Daniel 9,
Temba 7, Reggie 7

SCORERS:
Temba, Daniel x 3, Beardy Jake

WHAT WENT WELL:
1) We won
2) Daniel— scored a hat-trick
3) Our midfield finally played a FORWARD
   pass — hurray!

EVEN BETTER IF:
1) The Tigers could FOCUS! and not start
   showing off as soon as they go 3-0 up
2) Craig Crawley wasn't such a flushed
   football player
3) Coach Crawley wasn't such a friendly
   football manager

CHAPTER 11

FOOTBALL FOCUS

I felt like "The Real Deal" as I walked around the pitch after the final whistle, shaking hands with all the Magpies.

"Great game ... well played." It's waaaay easier being a good sport when you've just come up with the match-winning plan. Watch out, Paul Porterfield – there was a new football genius in Tissbury town!

But it turned out that Daniel wasn't the only one who was good at bursting my happy football bubble.

"I bet you're having a BALL, aren't you, Johnny?" Craig sneered as I went past. "You think you're so much better than Number 2! Well, enjoy this, waistcoat weirdo, because it won't last long. Not once I tell everyone who you really are..."

POP! Uh-oh, I was right – Craig 121 per cent DID know my secret! And I definitely didn't need to be an undercover football genius to work out who had told him. BILLY! I could even picture his great big grin as he bellowed it out:

You know who his brother is, don't you? DANIEL "THE CANNON" BALL!

Now that Craig knew about our secret brother bond, it was only a matter of time before he made his big announcement to the Tigers. But why was he so desperate to tell everyone? That night, when I couldn't sleep, I decided to make a really long list of possible reasons:

1) He doesn't like new people.

2) He doesn't like small(er) people.

3) He doesn't like people called Johnny.

4) He's jealous of my football genius.

5) He's just a really mean person.

6) He saw my "WAYS TO MAKE THE TISSBURY TIGERS (EVEN) BETTER" list and thinks that I'm trying to kick him off the team.

That last one seemed the most likely, especially when I thought carefully about what Craig had said to me after the match against the Magpies:

"You think you're so much better than Number 2!"

At first, I thought that he meant me wanting to

be the Tissbury Tigers manager instead of just the assistant – you know, Number 2 in charge. But what if he actually meant Number 2 on the team – you know, the right-back. That's what I had called Craig in the list I gave to Coach Crawley... And if he had read the list, then Craig probably did believe that I was trying to kick him off the team!

Which was kind of true. No, I hadn't written it down on my "WAYS TO MAKE THE TISSBURY TIGERS (EVEN) BETTER" list, but I had definitely thought it ... A ZILLION TIMES. Even though he hadn't been very nice to me, I still felt a tiny bit bad about that.

OK, well from now on, "Project Kick Craig Out" was officially over. It was time to go for a new tactic – I would call it ... "Project Be Kind to Craig". Although the Tigers would probably (definitely!) be better off without him (see, kinder already!), he was still part of the team. Plus, he knew my undercover secret, which I had to stop him from sharing with the other Tigers. Actually, maybe "Project Keep Craig Quiet" would be better...

Instead of working on his weaknesses (there were waaaay too many of those, anyway), I needed to find a way to work to Craig's strengths. So, what were they? I know, that's not an easy question to answer! Any ideas? What could we do in training that he would a) find fun and b) not be really bad at?

Think, Johnny, think!

When had I ever seen Craig look even a tiny bit happy?

TING! MINI LIGHT-BULB MOMENT.

Oh yeah, when he lobbed that ball at me as hard as he could!

TING! MAJOR LIGHT-BULB MOMENT.

Brilliant! Oh boy, I was proud of this one, because it was the perfect way to solve two problems with one great football idea. I could be kind to Craig and, at the same time, help make the Tissbury Tigers (even) better...

🏆 🏆 🏆

"DODGEBALL?!"

At first, Coach Crawley didn't seem as positive as usual, but don't worry, I soon persuaded him.

"What the Tigers need right now is FOCUS!" I explained. "You said it yourself when we let the Magpies back into the game last week. Well, you have to focus really hard in dodgeball, don't you? Because if you switch off for a second, a ball might smack you in the face!"

"OK great, let's give it a go!" Coach agreed after that.

When I told the Tigers, they thought it was the best idea ever. The chance to chuck stuff at each other? They were in. "Crossbar, I'm on Danny's team!"

"You're going south, suckerz!"

"Actually, I've chosen the two captains already," I said, my voice getting less squeaky-nervous with every word. "Noah … and Craig."

That news landed like a giant fun-sponge. At first, I could hear "HUMPH!"s all around the team huddle, but luckily, they didn't last long.

"Craig, you can pick first," I offered KINDLY.

I felt pretty confident about this part of my plan. Sure, the Tigers were all Football Gods, but remember, one stood out above the rest, like a tower of annoying super talent...

"Danny," Craig said, sort of smiling for once.

Job done! Our best and worst players would be on the same team. It was either going to be awesome ... or awful!

Once the last player had been picked (Aroon, in case you wondered), the two teams of five stood on either side of the pitch, with the balls lined up in the middle.

(Dev was off sick. He seemed to get sick a lot on Wednesdays, but then by the weekend, he was

always magically back for the match...)

"Ready, steady ... GO!"

I'll be honest, what followed was less like dodgeball and more like "do-what-you-want-with-the-ball". You see, in all my awesome master-planning, I had forgotten one thing – I didn't actually know any of the rules of dodgeball. Whoops!

Noah was the Tigers' goalkeeper, so he was great at diving towards the ball, but not so great at ducking out of the way of it. He was no match for the dream team...

"Ref! No way can Craig get that close to me!"

PLAY ON!

"Hey, Danny, that ball deffo hit you and you know it!"

PLAY ON!

When Coach Crawley blew the final whistle, the Tigers collapsed on the grass like moose after a marathon. So much chaos, so much concentration – they were exhausted!

But – and it was another big but, hehehe! – they were also ecstatic. Even Craig. Actually, especially Craig. Yes, he was enjoying his moment of glory, as the captain of the winning team. It was his rocket of a right arm that had led them to victory. I saw him and Daniel high-five as if they were BFFs now. It was weird watching my brother being nice for a change.

"Well done, everyone!" Coach Crawley cried out cheerfully. "Now we just need to turn that dodgeball focus into FOOTBALL focus!"

CHAPTER 12

A JAW-ON-THE-FLOOR MOMENT

TISSBURY TIGERS VS SLOPE HILL SLOTHS (PART 1)

After the drama of dodgeball, I was hoping to sit back, relax and watch a quiet game of football. Daniel and Craig were "teammatez" again, and the Tigers were playing the Slope Hill Sloths, who were officially the WORST team in the league. The scores at the top of the table looked like this

Position	Team	Played	Won	Drawn	Lost	Total
1	Cooperston Cobras	14	12	1	1	37
2	Tissbury Tigers	14	11	2	1	35

… and then dropped all the way down, like one of those super-scary theme-park rides…

Position	Team	Played	Won	Drawn	Lost	Total
10	Slope Hill Sloths	14	0	3	11	03

Wow, they hadn't won a single game all season! Surely the Tigers weren't going to need me and my undercover football genius against a team like the Sloths? They would thrash them any day of the week...

Even on the wettest, windiest most miserable day ever...

Even with Craig...

And even without Daniel!

Just joking. My super-talented big brother never missed a match, especially when there was a good chance of scoring a hat-trick, or two or three. Daniel was aiming to overtake Johnny "The Rocket" Jeffries as Tissbury's top scorer ever at youth level. Dad always said that it was "only a matter of time" before my brother broke The Rocket's record, but it was also "a matter of scoring twenty-three more goals".

So, could he score them all in one game against the Sloths? After sixteen seconds in the pouring rain, anything seemed possible.

Temba tapped it to Daniel. **BANG! SPLASH!** The ball landed in the six-yard box and skidded straight through the poor keeper's legs. 1–0 to the Tigers!

"That's my boy!" Dad started singing but then he swung his right leg too hard. "Owww, my ankle!"

It served him right for trying to out-embarrass Mum. Anyway, it was really important that the Tigers didn't get carried away like Dad. Had they learned their lesson from the match against the Magpies? It was time to test their football...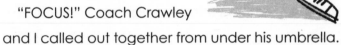

"FOCUS!" Coach Crawley and I called out together from under his umbrella.

And the Tigers actually listened to us! Even though they were winning already, they kept their concentration, and kept doing what they always did. Beardy Jake stayed at the back being big and strong, our midfield kept things simple and (mostly) sideways and Daniel went hunting for hat-tricks. Brilliant!

This time, it wasn't their focus that slipped; it was their odd one out...

The Sloths had worked out our weak link already. In the fifth minute, the manager moved a player over to the left wing.

I looked at Coach Crawley, but he just shrugged. "I've never seen that kid before – must be new!"

You didn't need to be a football genius to see the danger signs, though. The boy had fresh-from-the-box boots on his feet and "go faster" stripes shaved into his head.

Uh-oh. I could see Craig's shoulders slumping, and the new guy didn't even have the ball yet. When it finally came to him, Craig slow-mo charged in for the tackle and … NUTMEG!

That was embarrassing enough, but things were about to get even worse. As Craig turned around at the speed of a tortoise in a telephone box, he slipped and fell face-first into a massive pool of muddy water. The Sloths winger was away, splishing

and splashing towards the Tigers' penalty area, then *PING!* – top left bins – 1–1!

You know that super-awful sinking feeling you get in your stomach, when you realize something seriously not good is about to happen? Yeah, I had a really bad one of those right then. I looked over at Daniel and tried to send him an urgent mind-message, brother to brother: "No, no, no – you're teammates, remember? Please don't shout at—"

Too late.

"CRAIG, IF YOU DON'T FIX UP FAST, I SWEAR I'M GOING TO END YOUR FOOTBALL CAREER RIGHT HERE!"

No, no, no, no, NO! My brother was messing with the wrong rubbish footballer. What happened to the happy high fives? I had to stop him before Craig yelled something back—

Too late again.

"Whatevs, at least I'm better than YOUR BROTHER!" Craig spat, spraying out bits of mud and grass like a crazy cow.

GASP! Well, it was a "jaw on the floor" moment for me and Daniel anyway. The other Tigers just looked soaking wet and confused.

"What's he wafflin' about, Danny?"

"I didn't know you had a bro, mate. How come we've never seen him?"

Daniel and Craig stood there glaring at each other for aaaages, like boxers before a fight. The Sloths were now back in their own half, waiting for the match to restart, but the Tigers were going to need a "water break".

So, who would make the next move – Daniel or Craig? Unfortunately, it was Craig.

"Fine, if you won't tell them the truth, then I will. That waistcoat weirdo over there," he said, pointing at me, of course, "isn't called Johnny Bulawayo – no, he's called Johnny BALL! He's Danny's little brother."

GASP! This time, it was a "jaw on the floor" moment for all of the Tigers. The Football Gods were "flummoxed", as Grandpa George would say.

"Is he for real, Danny?"

"Maaaate, why would you duck on us about something dumb like that?!"

I looked over at my brother, who still hadn't said a word. His body was shivering with a weird mix of cold and fury. What was he going to do, now that our secret wasn't a secret any more? Would he be a good brother who had my back, or a bad brother who turned his back?

One thing was for sure: it was now game over for Johnny Ball: Undercover Football Genius.

CHAPTER 13

FOOTBALL OR FAMILY?

TISSBURY TIGERS VS SLOPE HILL SLOTHS (PART 2)

But before my brother could say or do anything, my parents decided to get involved ... both of them ... ON THE PITCH! Until that moment, I hadn't realized that you could be sick with super embarrassment, but trust me, you can.

"What's going on here then, lads?" Dad butted in, waving Mum's umbrella. "Come on, can't we just get on with the game and sort this out later?"

"No," said Daniel and Craig at exactly the same time.

"Not unless HE goes away!" Craig added, pointing at me again, of course.

"Johnny?" asked Mum and Dad at exactly the same time. Yes, me!

"Yeah, him – he's the problem around here!" said Craig.

"No, he ain't!" Finally, Daniel had found his voice again.

"Yeah, he is!" Craig was a boy on a mean mission.

"No, he ain't – you're the problem!"

"No, HE is!"

"No, YOU are!"

That went on and on for aaaages, like in the silly pantomime that Mum and Dad used to make us go to at Christmas.

Speaking of Dad, he just had to (big) but (hehehe!) in again, didn't he? "Laaaaaads, we're all on the same side he—"

"Not now, Steven," Mum pleaded, pulling him back and grabbing her umbrella at the same time. "You muscling in like this will only make things worse."

Well said, Mum! But actually, her words made things even worse. Because that made Dad determined to prove her wrong by saving the day.

"Johnny, why don't you stand back for a second?" he suggested. I could tell he was really angry, because his left ear was twitching. "Just while I get to the bottom of this."

"Absolutely not, Steven!" Mum shook her head firmly. "Johnny is just as much a part of this team as

Daniel. They'll all have to sort out their differences properly, here on the pitch." And before I could complain, she grabbed hold of my hand and gave it a squeeze. In front of EVERYONE. Thanks, but no, thanks, Mum!

"Liz, this is a big game for Daniel!" Dad argued back, out of the side of his mouth, snatching the umbrella again. A crowd of people had gathered around to watch, including the referee. And Craig, of course – he was loving our family fight.

"Well, Steven, Johnny's their assistant manager."

"But the Tigers need to win this one, Liz!"

"I know that, Steven, but I DON'T CARE!"

As Mum and Dad argued, the umbrella moved back and forth, from one to the other.

It was like watching a really terrible tennis match. In fact, it was turning into a proper – da da daaaa – SCENE!

The family side of my brain said, "Just take a step back like Dad says, Johnny. Then this will all stop!"

But the football side of my brain said, "Don't go, Johnny – this is what you're really good at! The Tigers need you and your great ideas."

Arghh, there was a terrible tug of war going on in my head...

"CAN EVERYONE PLEASE STOP YELLING!" I yelled.

Weirdly, that worked. Everything went quiet all over the football battlefield and everyone looked at me. Now I had to actually sort things out...

Family or football? Football or family?

Think, Johnny, think!

FWEEEEEEEEET! Saved by the whistle! I think the silence had suddenly reminded the referee that he was supposed to be in charge.

"Right, that's enough drama for one day," he growled. "The game must go on." Then he turned to my parents and reached into his shirt pocket. "You two, you're off!"

DOUBLE RED CARD!

"Now, wait a second, that's not—"

Dad was all ready to argue his "rights", but thankfully Mum dragged him away.

"Come on, Steven, I think we need to calm down."

Dad did go, but he grumbled all the way. Most of his words were lost in the wind, but here's what I did hear: "I'll ... angry ... letter ... league ... umbrella ... Liz."

"And you," the referee said, turning to point at me. Why did everyone keep doing that? Mum told me it was rude to point at people. "You've got one minute to sort this out, otherwise I'm sending you off too!"

Me? Why always me?

"Right, let's have a team vote!" Craig declared.

Wait, who had put him in charge?

"So, hands up who thinks Johnny should be allowed to carry on as the Tigers assistant manager? Remember, he's lied to us about who he really is and all he's done is make us mad."

His dad was meant to be the manager, not him!

I counted the hands as they went up.

One – Connor, our flying full-back...

Two – Reggie and his lush left foot...

Three – Aroon and his forward pass...

Four – Finn because he always does what Aroon does...

Five – Beardy Jake, our gentle giant!

Thanks, guys! I had helped them all, and now they were helping me.

I'm not that good at Maths, but there were eleven players on the team. Only five had voted for me... That meant there were six players left who wanted me to leave! I had surely already lost, but Craig still wanted to confirm his evil victory.

"OK, now hands up who thinks Johnny should be kicked off the team?"

The first hand shot up straight away.

One – Craig!

But after that, there was a long pause as the other players looked awkwardly at each other, shrugged and then let their hands creep up super slowly like the plants we grew last year with Miss Patel.

Two – "No Words, Just Nods" Noah...

Three – "Not Much of a Talker" Temba...

Four – "Team Joker" Tyler... "No hard feelz, yeah? Us Tigers gotta fight for that title, innit. We can't change our stripes now!"...

Five – "Dozy" Dev... (But only because "Cheating Craig" woke him up and then whispered something in his ear. I saw him!)...

And finally, six – Daniel, my own brother!

Daniel and Craig didn't agree about much, but apparently they agreed about getting rid of me. That really hurt. The others had probably only agreed with Craig so that they could get on with the game and then go home and get dry, but Daniel was different. He had decided to be a bad brother and turn his back on me. I would probably never forgive him for that. Ever.

"Well, well, well – 6–5!" Craig shouted out smugly. "I guess we're the winners and you, Johnny, are the loser. See you later, waistcoat weirdo!"

Really, that was it – one stupid vote and I was out? I looked over at Coach Crawley, but he just shrugged, smiled and said, "I'm sorry, JB – if that's what the team wants..."

"Fine, I'll go," I said with a heavy sigh, as rain trickled down my cheeks like tears. I wasn't crying, I promise, but it was a super-sad scene. "Good luck winning the league without me!"

I guess it was a silly thing to say, but I had to have the last word, didn't I? Oh well, my time at the Tissbury Tigers had been fun while it lasted. Right, where were Mum, Dad and their umbrella when I needed them?

I checked the car, but they weren't there.

I checked the changing room, but they weren't there either.

Eventually, I saw two heads peeking out through the trees at the edge of the pitch – one littler and one larger. So that was where my sent-off parents were sheltering!

"Psssst, over here, Johnny-jingle!"

"Sorry about all that, son. Football eh?! It won't happen again, we promise."

You can swap your football team, but you can't swap your family. My parents were so, sooooo embarrassing sometimes, but they were my parents. And, unlike Daniel, I could never stay mad at them for long. So the three of us huddled together to watch the second half through the trees.

"Do you want to talk about what happened, Johnny-pop?" Mum asked after a bit.

"Oh, I'll tell you later," I replied.

It wasn't the time for that now; the Tigers were having a total team meltdown!

Beardy Jake had become a big target man up front...

Daniel was now our midfield terrier, diving into angry tackles...

And Dev was just sitting in a puddle, watching the game go by.

"Nah, I'm not feeling it today," he said when Coach asked him politely to carry on playing.

WHAT. WAS. GOING. ON? It was like our Ball brother bombshell had destroyed the Tigers' team spirit. Suddenly they were all just playing for themselves out there. But hey, that's what happens when you fire your number one football genius!

Still, it was really hard for me to watch and not try to help the Tigers. They were my team and they needed me, even if they didn't know it yet.

Oh, and I haven't even mentioned Craig yet! He was playing a strange new position that I'll call "goal-line protector". Noah was still wearing the gloves, but he was now a sweeper keeper. He kept charging out of his box like a rhino on the run, leaving Craig behind to cover.

And here's the strangest part – Craig was actually doing a REALLY GOOD JOB! I know it's hard to believe, but it's true – I saw it with my own eyes. He stopped a series of Sloths shots with his long, thin ruler legs.

"Well done, Craig!" his dad cheered, forgetting that a) the team was playing terribly, and b) he was meant to be the manager.

Come on, Coach Crawley! Come on, you Tigers!

You see, even though I was mega angry at them for kicking me out, I still wanted them to win. They couldn't throw away the league title like this...

Sorry, Sloths, but the Tigers were super lucky that they were playing against a ... not-so-good team. And on a not-so-flat pitch too. You see, our opponents weren't called "Slope Hill" for nothing, and in the second half, the Tigers were kicking downhill...

Beardy Jake booted it long to Temba, who somehow managed to balance the ball on his boot, despite the wind. Wow, it was the most incredible control I had ever seen – was he using superglue or something?! Temba was already super fast, but with the wind pushing him down the hill, he looked like Usain Bolt with a "TURBO" button. **ZOOM!** He raced past the defender and then scooped the ball over the keeper. 2–1 to the Tigers!

See, teamwork and talent win the day, whatever the weather! Anyway, after that goal, the Sloths gave up big time. Their uphill struggle was over.

Aroon slipped a pass across to Temba. **BANG!** – through the keeper's legs – 3–1!

Reggie skated his way down the hill and then delivered a cross onto Daniel's head. **THUMP!** – back of the net – 4–1!

"Phew!" said Mum on one side of me, and "Phew!" said Dad on the other. But what about me in the middle? I didn't have a football team to (assistant) manage any more!

MATCH REPORT 3   🏁 JNB

TISSBURY TIGERS 4–1 SLOPE HILL SLOTHS

STARTING LINE-UP (MARKS OUT OF 10):
Noah 4, Craig 0, Connor 4, Beardy Jake 4,
Tyler 4, Finn 5, Aroon 5, Dev 5, Daniel 0,
Temba 6, Reggie 5

SCORERS:
Daniel x 2, Temba x 2

WHAT WENT WELL:
The Tigers won — that's all I've got

EVEN BETTER IF:
1) Craig Crawley hadn't told the Tigers about my undercover secret
2) My own brother hadn't betrayed me
3) I was still the Tissbury Tigers Assistant Manager

CHAPTER 14

TAKE ME BACK, TISSBURY PRIMARY (PLEASE)!

During the second half and then our horrible drive home, I did think about telling the truth and landing my big brother in big trouble, but in the end, I decided not to disobey Daniel's "demandz". What was the point? I would have to admit that I'd been kicked off the team, and it wasn't going to get my old job back.

So instead, I took a deep breath, opened my mouth and let out a six-word lie:

"Mum, Dad – I'm quitting the Tigers."

They were super surprised to hear that. So surprised that Dad stopped Tiss suddenly in the middle of the road and asked me to repeat it. After I'd said it again, there was total silence, as if I'd just revealed that I was actually an alien.

"But why, Johnny-bub? You love being the assistant manager," Mum said, doing her very worried face. "Is it because of what happened before, with Craig and Daniel? Sweetheart, I'm sure that was just a "heat-of-the-match" thing, whatever it was…"

"No, it's not that," I said, feeling my brother's sharp eye-darts shooting at me. Luckily, I already knew what I was going to say next. "I just miss coaching my friends."

"Well, son, that sounds like a sensible idea," Dad replied, looking more than a bit relieved.

Yes, it was time for me to go back to that angry first thought I had after reading Daniel's "demandz", waaaay back at the beginning. Remember? No, I didn't think so – that's why I've written it out again, in big, angry capital letters:

"FINE, WHATEVER, BRO, IF YOU DON'T WANT ME AROUND, I'LL JUST GO BACK TO BEING THE TISSBURY PRIMARY MANAGER THEN!"

🏆 🏆 🏆

It felt really weird being back at Tissbury Primary training after my time away with the Tigers. I reckon it's probably how an astronaut feels when they return to Earth after a wicked rocket trip to Mars.

It was a Wednesday night and so I should have been out watching my team of talented teenagers train, but instead I was secretly spying on a primary school practice through Miss Patel's classroom window (no, my undercover days weren't quite over yet!). Everything seemed so small – the pitch, the goals, and especially, the players. There wasn't a single beard in sight!

There was one thing that wasn't so small, though. Or maybe I should say "one person" – Mr Mann! If Tissbury Primary did take me back, he would still be the (not very good) manager, and I would be his assistant with all the ideas. No, not the BALL BOY – never listen to anything Billy says!

It would be one big step backwards for me, but oh well, it was better than nothing, right? At least then my great football ideas wouldn't go to waste, getting all mouldy in my brain-bin.

As I watched the Tissbury Primary training, it was like ABSOLUTELY nothing had changed. Mr Mann was still booming out the same silly football phrases:

COME ON, RUN YOUR SOCKS OFF!

NO, NO, NO – PUT IT IN THE MIXER!

GET STUCK IN!

Billy was still HOOF!ing the ball as hard as he could, often straight at his own teammates.

CLANK!

OWWW!

And Tabia was still beasting her way past everyone with her mad football skillz.

Tap-tap, flip-flap ... Maradona turn, Ronaldo chop ... and a weaker-foot Rabona to finish ...

GOAL!

TOO GOOD! Boy, Billy really didn't deserve to have a teammate like my best friend...

"Hey, why are you hiding inside, **SCAREDY-SQUID?**"

That wasn't Miss Patel talking by the way; she's too old and serious for nasty name battles. No, it was my football brain, asking me a very good question. Because I couldn't just stand there watching through the classroom window for ever. Eventually, I was going to have to go out there and ask Mr Mann for my Tissbury Primary: Assistant Manager job back.

Be brave, Johnny, be brave!

Fiiiiine! I waited until the session was over and Billy was back in the changing room, and then I crept outside. When I stepped onto the grass, suddenly the pitch seemed a whole lot bigger. I felt like I was crossing the Sahara Desert, not a primary school football field.

As Mr Mann watched me walking towards him, a smile spread across his face and he blew his body up even bigger. Yes, HE was the Big Boss-Mann around here, just in case I had forgotten.

"LOOK WHO'S BACK, TROOPS!" he boomed, even though Tabia was the only other person there. "THE FOOTBALL GENIUS WHO LEFT US BEHIND! BALLY JUNIOR, WHAT ARE YOU DOING HERE? LOOKING TO STEAL SOME OF MY BRILLIANT IDEAS FOR THE TIGERS, ARE YOU?"

Mr Mann's "brilliant ideas"? I had to squeeze my

face really hard to stop myself from laughing. That definitely wouldn't get my old job back.

"No, I–I, err," I started to say, but after that, my mind went blank. So much for Mission: Take Me Back, Tissbury Primary (Please)!

"SPIT IT OUT, BALLY JR!"

"Mr Mann, I was, err…"

Come on, Johnny, just say it!

"…wondering if I could have my old job back … please."

There, I'd said it – phew!

"WELL, WELL, WELL – LOOK WHO'S COME CRAWLING BACK, TROOPS!" Mr Mann boomed out with an even bigger grin bursting across his already bursting face. "IT TURNS OUT BALLY JUNIOR ISN'T TOO GOOD FOR US, AFTER ALL! WHAT DO YOU THINK – SHOULD WE LET HIM BACK IN?"

Who was he asking – himself? Yes, it must have been, because he answered his own question a few seconds later.

"SORRY, BALLY JUNIOR,

BUT WE'RE DOING JUST FINE WITHOUT YOU! WE WOULDN'T WANT TO UNSETTLE THE TROOPS NOW, WOULD WE, TABBY?"

All was not lost yet. I looked across at Tabia – she was always begging me to coach Tissbury Primary again. Well, here I was. Surely my best friend would help me get my old job back, right?

WRONG! Without even looking at me, she said, "I agree, Coach. We don't need Johnny."

Liar, liar, pants on fire! I couldn't believe it. First my brother, and now my best friend had betrayed me too. Was I the new most hated person in Tissbury?

"SORRY, BALLY JUNIOR – THE PLAYERS HAVE SPOKEN!" Mr Mann boomed a bit too cheerfully. "I GUESS YOU'LL NEED TO FIND A NEW TEAM, SEEING AS THE TIGERS DON'T WANT YOU ANY MORE EITHER."

I was back to where I'd started, back before I became an accidental football genius. I was hopeless and team-less. My dream of becoming "THE NEXT PAUL PORTERFIELD", the future number one football genius in the whole wide world was over.

As I plodded slowly and sadly off the pitch, I kept thinking, "How could Tabia do this to me?"

It didn't make sense. We were meant to be best friends, and best friends do NOT do that to each other. Ever. Everyone knows the order:

1) BEST FRIENDS

then

2) FOOTBALL.

But Tabia had decided that football was more important than me, and so our best friendship was over.

THE END.

Just kidding! It didn't turn out like that, because as I made my long, lonely way home, hating my ex-best friend under my breath, I suddenly heard a:

CLICK! CLACK!

It was coming from behind me, but when I turned around, the noise stopped. There was silence for a bit, but then I heard it again:

CLICK! CLACK!

What was going on? This time, as I turned, Tabia came sprinting around the corner towards me:

"We're into the last minute of the County Cup Final now, as Izzy dribbles the ball forward. Surely, Epic Forest are going to tackle her, but wait, LOOK! The other Tissbury Primary players have formed a ferocious line of lions to protect her..."

Oh right, that noise had been her kicking the most football-shaped stone that she could find. I knew what Tabia was trying to do, but it wasn't going to work.

"...they're up to the edge of the Epic penalty area now, with the goal in sight..."

It was time for my big Johnny "CAN Kick the" Ball moment, but for once, I didn't feel like playing. I wasn't just going to recreate THE GREATEST GOAL EVER with her and forget all about the horrible thing she had done. No way.

"Wait, *BUFFALO-BURP!*" Tabia called out. "Come on, don't be mad at me – I was just trying to help!"

What?! How did telling Mr Mann that Tissbury Primary didn't need me count as "trying to help"?

"Look, *DECIMAL-DOOFUS*, I did it for your own good. I don't know what's going on with the Tigers, but you're way too good to go back to Tissbury Primary. Do you really want to be Mr Mann's BALL BOY again? NO! You should be coaching the Tigers, not us, and you know it."

"But Craig doesn't want me there, and neither does Daniel!"

Tabia was ready for that rubbish answer. "So what? My mum doesn't want me to spend all my time playing football, but do I listen to her? NO! Instead, I listen to my grandma. She says that if you really want something, you shouldn't let anyone stop you!"

Old people are so wise, aren't they? I guess it's because they've seen a lot more things than the rest of us.

"Thanks, Tabs. I'll think about it," I muttered, managing a small smile. With our argument over, we walked home happily chatting the rest of the way. I guess that best, best friends are always trying to help, even if sometimes it doesn't seem that way at first.

Yes, I was feeling better already. Tabia was right – it was time for a ... CHANGE OF PLAN! I couldn't just give up on being Tissbury Tigers Assistant Manager. Not yet anyway, not without at least one attempt at an incredible comeback. But how was I going to do that, when the Tigers didn't even want me around?

A WEEKEND WITHOUT FOOTBALL

TISSBURY TIGERS VS PENCOT PENGUINS

Boy, weekends without football are BOOOOOORRRRRRING, aren't they?

That Saturday, after dropping Daniel and Dad off at the Tigers' next match (against the Pencot Penguins, in case you care), Mum and I headed off to do – da da daaaa – A BIG SUPERMARKET SHOP.

YAWN! Yes, now that I didn't have a football team to (assistant) manage, this was what my sad life had come to.

"I just think it's such a shame that you don't want to coach the Tigers any more," Mum said, only half-letting me push the trolley, even though everyone knows that's the only fun part of being at the supermarket. "You were doing a really brilliant job, Johnny-jim-jams! But I do understand – you must miss Tabia and the others."

What she didn't know yet was that I wasn't welcome at Tissbury Primary either. Oh well, that could wait; for now, I was stuck in the super-embarrassing experience of shopping with my mum.

"Anyway, it's so nice to have your help, honeybun!" she said, handing me half of the shopping list. It was the half without the chocolate, crisps and cereal on it (Mum knows me too well) and it was nearly as long as Grandpa George's super-long scarf.

Nooooo, why had I said yes to this?! I had never even heard of half the things:

Were they even real things you could eat?

> self-raising flour (what, did it wake up without an alarm?)
> courgettes (not cucumbers?)
> kale (more like "fail"!)
> nutmeg (wait a minute, that's a football move!)
> kaloobidoobydoo

OK, I did make that last one up, but still, how was I supposed to find the items when I didn't know what they were, let alone what they looked like?

After ten minutes of trying, I gave up. I handed my half of the list back to Mum with a "Sorry!" and went to look at the magazines instead. But my mind was still somewhere else: at a certain football match...

"Can we go now?" I asked, like a really annoying little toddler. The only thing missing was the yanking on the sleeve. As you can tell, I wasn't coping well without football.

Mum smiled. "Sure thing, kiddo. Whatdya wanna do instead?" she asked, putting on her awful American accent.

Hmm, good question! Basically, anything but supermarket shopping ... oh and watching my old team, the Tigers, play. I wasn't ready for that yet.

In the end, we settled for a quick kickaround in the garden (goals scored past Mum 1, balls booted over into Mrs Taylor's garden 3), followed by my favourite film ever: "JOHNNY 'THE ROCKET' JEFFRIES PRESENTS ... FOOTBALL'S FUNNIEST FAILS!"

Ha ha ha ha ha ha ha – hilarious!

So I was having a pretty good afternoon, actually, UNTIL...

THUD! ... STOMP! STOMP! STOMP!

As soon as I heard that car door slam (poor Tiss!), I just knew that something bad had happened at the Tigers match. Daniel stormed straight past Mum and up to his bedroom, where he slammed another door behind him. *THUD!*

"Oh dear, did they lose, Steven?"

"No," Dad shook his head and sighed very seriously. "They drew ... 0–0."

No wonder Daniel was slamming doors! That was his worst nightmare – not winning and not even scoring in the same match. But how? The Penguins weren't even that good, were they? I looked at the league table:

Position	Team	Played	Won	Drawn	Lost	Total
5	Pencot Penguins	15	3	9	3	18

OK, so the Penguins did really like a draw, but still, this was Daniel, "one of the best young players that our town has ever seen"! How had he failed to score a single goal against them? Something was wrong ... very wrong.

Eventually, Dad managed to drag Daniel down for dinner, but he still wasn't speaking. And after eating a few slices of pizza, he was about to storm back upstairs, when suddenly there was a knock at the front door.

"Who could that be?" Mum asked as she went to answer it.

(This is your chance to take a guess, while I

quickly creep over to the door and take a peep.)

It was...

Beardy Jake ... and Temba!

(Well done if you got it right, but I bet you didn't!)

"Oh, hi, boys, are you here to see Daniel?"

"Hi, Mrs Ball," Temba said super politely. "Sorry to disturb you at dinner time. No, we're actually here to see Johnny."

"Johnny?" Mum sounded surprised and so was I as I sat at the table, listening in. Why me? I looked over at Daniel, but he was staring down at his plate.

"Yes, is Johnny home, please?" Temba asked. He had already said more words at our front door than during all our training sessions put together.

"Of course," Mum replied, sounding more and more confused, "come in, boys ... JOHNNY, YOU'VE GOT VISITORS!"

Not for the first time during my football manager adventure, I was asking myself, "WHAT IS GOING ON?" But weirdly, I didn't feel worried this time – not even a little bit. The Tigers now knew who I really was, so I had nothing left to hide. In fact, I could feel my hope rising upwards, like steam from a teapot.

Thankfully, Temba got straight to the point, once he had shut the living room door so that my family couldn't hear us: "Johnny, we need you back ... NOW!"

"Yeah, sorry, J – we're not the same team without you!" Beardy Jake backed him up.

Woah, I was right – things must have gone spectacularly wrong against the Penguins!

"What happened in the match?" I asked.

"Well, it all started when Danny missed an easy one-on-one at the end of the first half, and you know how mad he gets when that happens."

(Yeah, like a hippo with a sore head! Sorry, carry on, Temba…)

"Then, in the second half, it just got way worse. You know how kick-off works, right? One player has to pass it to another player. Well, Danny passed it … to himself! The ref gave a free kick to the Penguins and that just made him even madder.

After that, he just charged around the pitch, barging people off the ball – even us, his own teammates! Coach Crawley tried to calm him down, but you know what he's like."

(Yeah, way too friendly to be a top football manager! Sorry, carry on, Temba…)

"Man, it was so simple for the Penguins defence – all they had to do was mark one guy! Danny just kept taking stupid shots from the halfway line and trying to dribble the ball into the net on his own. Surprise, surprise, he didn't score – duuuuuh!"

"Yeah, basically, your ball-hog bro ruined it for the rest of us!" Beardy Jake burst out.

"Sorry, Johnny, we made a big mistake when we kicked you out of the team," Temba said, taking over the talking again. "We need you and your great football ideas back, otherwise we've got no chance of winning the league now!"

"WELL, WELL, WELL – LOOK WHO'S COME CRAWLING BACK!" my brain boomed in its best Mr Mann voice. I didn't say that out loud, though, because it was nice to feel wanted again. Was this the incredible comeback that I'd been hoping for? I did really want my old job back, but I could already see two problems with Temba's plan.

1) "What about Craig – does he know you're here?"

Beardy Jake swatted the air with his big, strong hand, as if Craig was just an annoying fly, rather than a flushed but human-sized footballer.

"Not yet, but we'll deal with him later. We'll have another team vote at training, and this time, you'll win for sure."

2) "OK, and what about my brother – does he know about this?"

"DANNY! CAN YOU COME IN HERE?" Temba shouted.

As he entered the room, I had never seen my brother look so miserable before, not even that time he'd got really sick and couldn't play football for three whole weeks.

Daniel already knew most of what was coming next, but even he looked surprised to hear it coming from Temba's mouth:

"Right, what happened against the Penguins can't happen again, gottit? I know you think you're way better than the rest of us, but you've got to pass the ball next time. The Tigers are a TEAM – we've got to play TOGETHER. That's how football works, mate!"

Daniel looked like he'd never heard the game described like that before. "But why'd you never say nothing until now, T?" he asked. "We've been teammatez for years!"

"Yeah, but you were never this bad before, and there wasn't a league title on the line. Anyway, how was I supposed to say something when you never shut up and let me speak?"

Well, that did the job! Daniel had to swallow his words and his pride.

"And one more thing," Temba carried on. "We want Johnny back, and he's agreed, just as long as you're OK with it. Deal?"

It wasn't easy for my brother to admit when he was wrong, but what choice did he have?

"Deal," Daniel agreed at last, with an angry glare. As we shook on it, he squeezed really hard and crushed my knuckles.

Arghh! He had been winning brother battles like that for years. But this time, we both knew he had lost.

MATCH REPORT 4   ✏ JNB

TISSBURY TIGERS 0—0 PENCOT PENGUINS

STARTING LINE-UP (MARKS OUT OF 10):
Noah, Craig, Connor, Beardy Jake, Tyler, Finn, Aroon, Dev, Daniel, Temba, Reggie — 0 out of 10 (because I wasn't there)

SCORERS:
None!

WHAT WENT WELL:
Nothing much (other than me getting my old assistant manager job back, of course!)

EVEN BETTER IF:
Remember, I wasn't there, so I'm only guessing, but:
1) The Tigers had scored a goal
2) The Tigers had played well
3) The Tigers had won the game
4) The Tigers hadn't got rid of their number one football genius — but don't worry, I'm back!

CHAPTER 16

TEAM-BUILDING WITH THE TIGERS

You know how in the best films the heroes always arrive at exactly the right moment to save the day? Well, that's what I was going to do at the next Tissbury Tigers match. And I had picked the perfect time to make my assistant manager return: the DENNIS THE DONKEY DERBY!

That's right, with two games to go in the season, we were up against our biggest rivals, the Rockley Raptors.

BOOOOOOOOOOOOOO!
HISSSSSSSSSSSSSSSSS!

Sorry, here's a quick local history lesson for you:

The story goes that back in ancient times (when Grandpa George was still quite young) there was this donkey called Dennis who liked to trot the streets and fields of Tissbury and Rockley. Dennis was a big football fan, or at least a big fan of eating all the grass around a football pitch, anyway.

Dennis loved both towns and both towns loved him. Sometimes he'd watch a game in Tissbury and sometimes he'd watch a game in Rockley. It was all fair and friendly until, one day, Bert Bagstaff, the Rockley Rovers manager, declared that Dennis was officially their donkey. They gave him a team shirt and paraded him around the pitch before kick-off.

Woah, the Tissbury Town fans were furious. Dennis wasn't Rockley's donkey; he was football's donkey! And from that day on, the two teams became really fierce rivals.

Rockley Rovers' kit colour? Dennis the Donkey grey.

Tissbury Town's kit colour? Delicious grass green.

Rockley's nickname? The Donkeys.

Tissbury's nickname? The Dennises.

One time, a massive soft toy donkey was even thrown onto the pitch during a Dennis the Donkey Derby match, and the players started fighting over it. Mum won't let us go to those games any more because she says they're "too dangerous".

And it's not just the senior teams who don't like each other. It's the same in the younger age groups too: the Tissbury Tiger Cubs vs the Rockley Raptor Hatchlings and the Tissbury Tigers vs the Rockley Raptors.

THE END

So now you know why the Tigers needed to be at their "No 'I' in TEAM!" best for the big Dennis the Donkey Derby. Remember, we had to win, otherwise the title race was over. So there was no way that we could play like we had against the Magpies, or the Sloths, or the Penguins. If we did, the Raptors would tear us into tiny little pieces!

They were a really tough team to beat and they had just jumped ahead of the Weston Warthogs into third place in the league table:

Position	Team	Played	Won	Drawn	Lost	Total
1	Cooperston Cobras	16	14	1	1	43
2	Tissbury Tigers	16	12	3	1	39
3	Rockley Raptors	16	8	6	2	30

Plus, we were playing the Raptors away at Crater Park, where they hadn't lost a single match in six whole seasons.

So, what could I do to help the Tigers?

Think, Johnny, think!

The pressure was on, but boy did it feel good to be back– doing what I did best – using my great football ideas to win football matches. And best of all, now that I wasn't undercover any more, I could just be me – Johnny Ball, Assistant Manager, "THE NEXT PAUL PORTERFIELD", the future number one football genius in the whole wide world!

Yes, I was finally free to wear whatever I wanted...

Bye, bye, Tigers hat! Hello again, favourite red tracksuit! Ahhh, much better. I felt comfortable in my own skin, and my own "saddo" scarf, again.

And I was also free to concentrate on more important assistant manager-y things, like FOCUS and TEAMWORK!

Teamwork was super important. Tissbury Primary would NEVER have won the County Cup if our players hadn't worked together. The Tissbury Tigers had waaaay more talent (sorry, but it's true!), but some of them – not naming names *COUGH* my brother *COUGH* – were clearly playing for themselves, and not for the team. Our only chance of winning the Dennis the Donkey Derby was to all work together, even Daniel and even Craig.

That's why, once I'd been voted back in at training (ten yesses, one no – you won't need to be a football genius to guess who that was!), I said to Coach Crawley that maybe we should do a quick bit of Tigers team-building stuff before the big game.

"Great, let's give it a go!" he replied in his usual really friendly way. "Welcome back, by the way – we really missed you. So, what would you like them to do?"

Wait no! I didn't have a proper plan yet – that's why I used the word "stuff"!

Never mind, TEAM-BUILDING...

Think, Johnny, think!

What did Daniel like doing? I made a quick list in my pocket notebook:

1) Being moody
2) Wearing headphones (with or without the music playing)
3) Paintballing
4) Online gaming
5) Messaging really, really fast
6) Doing wheelies on his BMX bike

No, none of those would work! It would have to be one of my greatest football ideas ever – something so sneaky, clever and fun that a) the Tigers would all (including Craig) think, "Wow, I'm so glad that we brought Johnny back – he's BRILLIANT!" and b) Daniel wouldn't even notice that I was breaking one of his "demandz": 5) Don't EVER try to coach ME.

So how could I coach my brother without him knowing he was being coached? It was going to be difficult, but at least it wouldn't be my first time as an undercover football genius!

I wrote "TEAM-BUILDING" in big letters in a big bubble in the middle of a new page, and then waited for all my great ideas.

When nothing arrived, I just stared at the word for a while:

TEAM-BUILDING ... building ... a team...

TING! LIGHT-BULB MOMENT. Daniel loved playing FIFA and fantasy football too. He always picked the best players and came top of our family league. So what if we made the Tigers team-building exercise all about building the ultimate 5-a-side football team! Surely, even moody teenagers would find that fun...

Most of those questions came from Daniel, who seemed super keen all of a sudden. Well, except the

"OK, what's the prize if we win?" was the first question and there were lots more to come:

CAN WE CHOOSE ANY FORMATION?

DO THE PLAYERS STILL HAVE TO BE PLAYING?

DO THEY STILL HAVE TO BE ALIVE?

ARE YOU THE JUDGE, BECAUSE YOU'RE WELL YOUNG AND YOU PROBS DON'T KNOW FUDGE ABOUT FOOTBALL?

last one – he already knew that I know a lot more than "fudge" about football.

"Coach Crawley and I will be the judges," I said, trying to sound like I'd made the game up months ago, instead of at that moment. "You can choose any formation and any footballer ever. There's only one rule: each of you must pick one of the players and talk about why. Oh, and the winners will get ... a special, secret prize."

Nope, no one was falling for that.

"Right, here are the groups..."

TEAM 1: Daniel, Craig, Jake, Aroon, Reggie.

TEAM 2: Noah, Temba, Finn, Tyler, Connor.

(Dev was sick – AGAIN!)

"...your ten minutes start ... NOW!"

At first, it was like the start of playtime at Tissbury Primary. Everyone tried to talk at the same time, but some voices were louder than others...

"Right, we've gotta have Johnny Jeffries up top!" Daniel declared. "No doubtz – total ledge. And then Nigel Andrews in nets—"

"Wait, we get one pick EACH." Beardy Jake was the one who stood up to my brother, probably because he was the biggest and strongest. "It's not all about you, Golden-Ball!"

"Whatevs. Let's hear which wasters you lot want, then?"

Reggie: "We'll need some mad skillz in attack, so I pick Donaldinho. He's a 99 rating on FIFA and they don't call him the Mayor of Flair for nothing. His flip flap is BRAAAAAP!"

Daniel: cool-kid nod of respect.

Aroon: "In the middle, it's Kevin Akintola for me. He can run all game long and he's rapid, so he could play in defence and midfield. It's like having two guys for the price of one, innit!"

Daniel: cool-kid nod of respect.

Jake: "At the back, I'll go for Marcel Maison. No one's messing with that monster!"

Daniel: cool-kid nod of respect.

And last but never least, Craig: "Err, I was thinking, like, José Rico in nets? Because he makes super saves and he's a sick sweeper keeper … maybe."

Daniel: pause, another pause, then cool-kid nod of respect.

Wow, how easy was that? Team 1's ultimate 5-a-side football team was sorted, without a single strop or "savage" word. Maybe my brother's teammates weren't so "flushed" when it came to football, after all. I just had to hope that Daniel would now remember that in the heat of the football match too.

Over in Team 2, the Tigers were sitting in a nice, quiet circle, LISTENING to each other. Can you believe it? It was so … peaceful. One by one, they picked their player and gave their reasons why. No mocking, no "mad banter". It was amazing – Temba's answer was like a two-thousand word essay, and I even heard Noah and Connor speak for at least thirty seconds each!

Mission: Tigers Team-building – COMPLETE!

It didn't really matter which group won, so in the end, we sweet-chilli-chickened out and called it a draw.

"Who cares? We're all on the same team anyway, remember!" Coach Crawley cried out cheerfully.

CHAPTER 17

TIGER TRAIN TO THE RESCUE

TISSBURY TIGERS VS ROCKLEY RAPTORS

"Come on, let's go wreck those Raptors!" Daniel yelled out as we all arrived at Crater Park TOGETHER.

"YEAH!" the other Tigers all joined in, even Craig.

Hurray, my plan was working; they were acting like a team again. First, we would win the Dennis the Donkey Derby, and then the league title. Talent? Tick! Passion? Tick! Focus? Tick! Togetherness? Tick! The Tigers had everything they needed now, so what could possibly go wrong? Plenty of things, as it turned out.

"Happy Derby Day, JB!"

"Happy Derby Day, Coach!"

The sun was shining, and the supporters were singing. Although Crater Park was mostly full of Raptors fans, it was the small group of Tigers fans who were making the most noise.

He scores goals, he's my son, he is always number one, DANNY BALL! DANNY BALL! We love you, Johnny, we do, We love you, Johnny, we do!

Woah, new levels of super embarrassment, although at least everyone knew that we were brothers now!

As the match kicked off, the atmosphere was really, really tense. For the first ten minutes, both teams tiptoed around the pitch playing short, boring passes because everyone was terrified of making a mistake on DERBY DAY. It was a bit like in our class at school when someone does a super-stinky fart, and no one wants to admit it was them.

He who smelt it, dealt it!

She who did the rhyme, did the crime!

Anyway, back to the football. We needed someone to step up and be brave out there, and of course, that someone turned out to be Daniel. Just to be clear: he didn't own up to a tremendous trump; he scored a great goal. 1–0!

Get in! Right, now that my super-talented big brother had given us the lead, it was time to test that team spirit. Could the Tigers now work together to hold on and win the Derby?

All over the pitch, our players upped their games:

Noah was now more "Safe Hands", and less "Wild Sweeper Keeper"...

Beardy Jake turned on his monster mode, doing his best Marcel Maison impression at the back...

Aroon was everywhere in midfield, as if he was Kevin Akintola himself...

Finn had discovered that he could do forward passes too...

On the wing, Reggie was doing tricks that even the great Donaldinho didn't know...

And up front, Daniel and Temba were leading the team fearlessly, like two Johnny "The Rocket" Jeffries.

It was so good to see all of the Tigers hitting top form together. Well, all of them except Dev. He was supposed to be playing right wing, but he might as well have been right back in the changing room for all the running and dribbling he was doing.

What was going on with him? Didn't he want to win the league title? Where were his usual silky skillz? The sleepy eyes, the sneaky naps, the training sessions off "sick", that sit-down against the Sloths … something was definitely up with Dev and it was my job to find out what. Amazingly, that was the only thing on my "HALF-TIME TASKS" list, right up until the very last minute of the first half.

That's when the Raptors really went for our weak spot. I guess they had played against Craig enough times to know that he wasn't very good at … well, at football, full stop.

So when the Raptors left-winger finally got the ball, he decided to lead Craig on a dizzying little dance:

Stepover to the left, stepover to the right…

Stepover to the left, stepover to the right…

CRISS-CROSS! CRISS-CROSS!

After a minute of watching feet flipping and flapping all over the place, Craig looked like he might topple over. In the end, Beardy Jake had to come over and **BOSH!** the winger off the ball. Free kick to Rockley! Their massive central midfielder took a massive run-up and **THUMP!** – crossbar and in – 1–1!

Arghh, that super-awful sinking feeling again – just when everything had been going so well! Never mind, I tried to focus on the good stuff:

1) The Tigers were playing together like a proper team.

2) Daniel hadn't got angry at anyone yet, not even Craig after the Raptors equalised.

And...

3) We had half-time to regroup and put my great football ideas into action.

"Oh good, I'm so glad you've got some great ideas, Johnny!" you're probably thinking right now. But actually, they were running a little late. Hurry up, brain! While I waited for them to arrive, I decided to try and speak to Dev.

"Can you help me ... fill up the water bottles quickly?" I asked him. I'll admit it; that wasn't the best offer ever.

He let out a really loud sigh. "Soz, J, but I'm all out of gas. Can't Craig do it?"

"No, come on, you only need to carry one."

"Fine!" Zombie Dev said, slowly following me to the changing room.

Right, this was my big moment, our chance to speak man to man(ager). Number one football geniuses like Paul Porterfield always know how to talk to their players and get them back to their best.

"So what's up, D?" I was trying my hardest to sound super cool and casual.

"Just a bit busted – that's all, J."

Change of plan – I didn't have time to take it nice and slow. Dev had been acting weird for weeks. I had to go straight in with the difficult question:

"You can be honest with me, you know – I won't tell the others. What's really going on?"

Dev looked at me for aaaages, as if he was trying to work out whether he could trust me with the truth. Of course, he could! Ask Tabia – I'm so good at keeping secrets.

"Promise you won't tell the Tigers?"

Me: nod.

Dev: deep breath... "I'm inescoomply."

"Sorry, what?" I couldn't hear the last part because Dev mumbled it into his shirt.

He looked around for spies – nope, the coast was clear. "I said, I'm in the school play."

"Oh, congratulations!"

"Thanks, J, but it's way more work than I thought it would be. I've got the lead role, you see, and there's so much speaking and singing AND dancing..."

(A-ha, so that's where Dev's magic moves had disappeared to!)

"...and I have to go to rehearsals every night after school..."

(And that was why Dev had been missing so many Tissbury Tigers training sessions!)

"...my life is miserable, man! By the time I get to the weekend, I'm too tired for football. I was up until 3 a.m. learning my lines! How wack is that?"

That was really, really wack. But what could I do to help Dev?

"What if Coach Crawley speaks to the drama teacher?" I suggested. There was no way that they were going to listen to the nine-and-a-quarter-year-old assistant manager. "Maybe they could make a deal, so that you can still be brilliant at both?"

"Yeah, maybs that could work, lil man." Dev nodded. "It's worth a try for sure. Cheers, J – it's good to chat deep sometimes, innit. I feel better already."

No problem! Right, time to move on to my next, much trickier half-time task – what was I going to do about Craig? I know, I know – I had been putting off that problem for waaaay too long.

It wasn't (all) his fault that the Raptors had scored, but Craig was our weak spot and if I didn't do something soon, our rivals would come back for more, our title dream would be over, and so would my incredible comeback as Tissbury Tigers Assistant Manager.

UNLESS...

No, we couldn't take him off because then we would be down to ten men. Craig was bad, but he was better than no one, surely?!

Think, Johnny, think!

What if we moved Craig to a safer place on the pitch? *TING! LIGHT-BULB MOMENT.*

I whispered my plan to Coach Crawley.

"Are you sure?" he asked at first, but he didn't have a better idea. Or any idea, actually. "OK great, let's give it a go!"

Apparently, that meant it was my turn to give … THE SCARY HALF-TIME TEAM TALK. I took a quadruple-deep breath because Daniel really wasn't going to like what I was about to do.

"Right, w-we're going to make a few … changes," I said, suddenly sounding not very sure. "Dev, you're going to move to right-back, Temba you're going to move to right wing…"

I could see the Tigers trying to work out what was coming next.

"…and Craig, you're going up front with Daniel."

He glared, he groaned, he hugged his arms really tightly, but my brother didn't say anything. That's because even Daniel knew that it was for the best. Keeping Craig up front would be keeping Craig – and the Tigers – out of trouble.

"Look, he thinks he's a striker now!" The Raptors left-winger pointed and laughed as the second half started.

But he wasn't laughing so hard when Not-so-zombie Dev and Beardy Jake double-tackled him every time. Yeah, TIGERS TEAMWORK!

The good news was that we now looked waaay more solid at the back; the bad news was that we now looked waaaay less awesome in attack. Daniel and Craig were playing like strangers, not super-strike partners.

I did feel a tiny, tiny bit bad for my brother. Swapping Temba with Craig was like swapping a lovely slice of cake for the lumpy cauliflower cheese they give us at school. No, thank you! Daniel didn't know what to do – should he become a ball hog again like against the Penguins, or pass it to Craig and probably never get it back?

Time was running out and, remember, we HAD to win the Dennis the Donkey Derby…

"Come on, Tigers, we can still do this!" Coach Crawley cheered nervously next to me. "You don't have any more of your great ideas, do you Johnny? We could really use one right now!"

I didn't, but Temba did. Well, actually it was a joint idea, really – the two of us working together. As he came over to take a throw-in, he muttered five magical words to me:

"What about the Tiger Train?"

TING! TEMBA AND JOHNNY'S JOINT LIGHT-BULB MOMENT.

"Of course! Why didn't I think of that? Thanks, T!"

Oooh the TIGER TRAIN – sounds super cool, right? It was a secret move that we had worked on after training. Well, some of us, anyway...

You see, there was nothing that I could do about our awful new attack. Daniel wasn't going to let me coach him, and neither was Craig. But the Tiger Train was perfect because it was a great football idea that didn't involve either of them.

Coach Crawley liked our idea – of course, he did! – and so I grabbed Dev as quickly as I could. This time, I didn't even bother with the whispering:

"This is your moment. I don't care how you do it, but you need to win a corner kick!"

"Gottit, JB!"

How did Dev do it? With those silky skillz that I was telling you about earlier! Thanks to our deep chat, he was back to his best, dribbling the ball all the way from way back in our own half, and then booting it against the defender's leg. Beautiful!

"Great work, Dev!" I cheered. Then as Reggie came over to take the corner, I whispered to him, "Time for the TIGER TRAIN!"

"Sweet!" As he ran up to curl the ball into the box with his lush left foot, Reggie suddenly called out, "CHOO! CHOO!"

Beardy Jake was waiting in the box near the penalty spot and he heard it loud and clear. "ALL ABOARD!" he boomed back.

In a flash, the other player-passengers formed a line behind and in front of him: Tyler and Temba in front, Aroon and Finn behind. See, a Tiger Train!

The Raptors looked sooooo confused, but not as confused as Craig – or Daniel, who was being double-marked at the back post. What was going on? Why weren't they in on the plan? Oh well, they were both the odd ones out now!

When the corner came in, most of the Tiger Train split off in different directions, followed by desperately chasing Raptors defenders. But the gentle giant in the middle hadn't moved at all, and Beardy Jake was now unmarked as the ball flew towards his big head.

THUD!
GOOOOOAAAAALLLLL!!!!!
2–1!

Sorry, I know I said I wasn't going to do the running knee slide until we won the league title, but I couldn't help it. Plus, I wasn't the only one doing it.

"Johnny, you're a genius!" Temba shouted as we celebrated together. We made a pretty awesome team.

"No, you are – top work, T!"

Our great football idea had worked perfectly. We were about to win the Dennis the Donkey Derby!

"All aboard the TIGER TRAIN!" I screamed up into the sky above Crater Park and then before I knew it, I was even doing a little "CHOO CHOO!" dance to go with it. Luckily, Mum had left her phone at home that day, so there is no video evidence.

There were only a few minutes left after that, and our defence stood strong against the Raptors attack. At the final whistle, The Tigers jumped for joy all over the field. What a derby victory, and we deserved it too! I wasn't going to join in the team celebrations, I promise, but Beardy Jake made me, and he's really big and strong.

"J, I'm just gonna say it – you're a flippin football GENIUS!" he yelled, putting his sweaty, beardy face right up to my ear. "It's great to have you back, lil man. You Ball Brothers, eh? Class!"

Wow, what a kind thing to say, and now it would be ringing in my ears for weeks! That pushed me up to eleven on the proud-of-myself scale, and things were about to get even better.

"Have you heard the news?" Noah's dad called out. It was a silly question really, seeing as we'd all been watching/playing a football match. "The Cobras only drew with the Warthogs!"

"Get in!" we all cheered together, like a proper football team.

The title race wasn't over yet! My relief mixed with my excitement and bubbled over like a fizzed-up lemonade fountain. Because that meant that, with one game to go, the top of the league table looked like this:

Position	Team	Played	Won	Drawn	Lost	Total
1	Cooperston Cobras	17	14	2	1	44
2	Tissbury Tigers	17	13	3	1	42

And who were the Tigers playing in their final game of the season? Yep, you guessed it – the Cobras ... at home!

Oh boy, this was going to be the biggest game EVER, and there was no way that I was going to miss it.

MATCH REPORT 5   🐯 JNB

TISSBURY TIGERS 2–1 ROCKLEY RAPTORS

STARTING LINE-UP (MARKS OUT OF 10):
Noah 8, Craig 5 (kinder!), Connor 8,
Beardy Jake 9, Tyler 8, Finn 8, Aroon 8,
Dev 7 (much better in the second half!),
Daniel 9, Temba 8, Reggie 8

SCORERS:
Daniel, Beardy Jake

WHAT WENT WELL:
1) We won!!
2) The Cobras drew, so we can still win the title!
3) We showed spirit to fight back and win
4) Daniel didn't shout at anyone all game
5) Our teamwork was terrific. All aboard the TIGER TRAIN!!!

EVEN BETTER IF:
1) Craig Crawley wasn't such a flushed football player
2) Coach Crawley wasn't such a friendly football manager
3) I wasn't just the assistant manager

CHAPTER 18

THE BATTLING BALL BROTHERS

"Ooooooo I'm so proud of my two Tissbury Tigers!" Mum squealed from the front seat, her fingers pinching invisible cheeks. Luckily, I was in the back of the car and out of reach.

"Thanks!" I said, turning to my brother next to me. "What a game, eh, Daniel?"

I was still buzzing, and I thought that my brother would be too. But no, I thought wrong.

"Whatevs," he grunted and that was the only word he said all journey.

"Daniel, darling, what—" Mum began to ask, but Dad gave her a "leave it!" look. As soon as Tiss stopped outside our house, my brother stomped upstairs and slammed another door behind him.

I didn't get it – why was he sooooo annoyed? And why now, when everything was going so well? Daniel had scored our first goal in the game, the

Tigers had won the Dennis the Donkey Derby, and we could still win the league. So WHY all the evil eye-darts and slamming doors?

Mum had a simple answer for Daniel's bad mood:

"Teenagers, eh!" she said with a sigh, as if that word explained everything. "Don't worry, love – and well done for today. Was that line thing all your own idea, darling?"

It was called the Tiger Train and yes, of course, it was all my own idea – I was a football genius! Not that some people seemed to care about that...

So far, Daniel's big huff had only managed to squish my happy football bubble a bit. There was waaaay worse to come, though.

When I went up to my room and opened the door, I felt a *SCRUNCH!* below my feet. I got that super-awful sinking feeling straight away because I knew exactly what it was.

I had stepped on a folded piece of paper that looked like it had been torn out of a school exercise book. And there was a letter scrawled pretty badly on the front: J.

This time, he hadn't even bothered to leave the note on my pillow. Apparently, Daniel was so angry at me that he couldn't even bear to step inside my room any more, let alone say whatever he wanted to say to my face.

J,

CHANGE OF PLAN – don't get me wrong, you could probs be a killer coach somewhere else, but NOT at the Tigers. Soz, just saying. U + ur team-work talkz are cramping my style, Bro. This title race is too tight for the both of us, so one of us is gonna have to go.
(That's u. I was here first, plus I'm the super-star striker, innit.)
See ya around the house. Don't hate on me, Bro.
Danny B

POP! My happy football bubble burst, right in my happy football face. Just when I was getting on so well with the other Tigers; just when I was really helping to make them a better team; and just when I was proving myself as "THE NEXT PAUL PORTERFIELD", the future number one football genius in the whole wide world. Boy, my brother sure knew how to ruin my life with one nasty little letter.

But wait a second – I didn't have to just do what Daniel said any more, did I? The days of his "demandz" were over! The Tigers now knew that I was his brother and they didn't mind at all. THEY had asked ME to come back as assistant manager, so why should I listen to my brother and his stupid letter?

"Here," I said, handing it back to him at the dinner table.

"What's that?" Mum asked straight away. She never missed a thing.

"Nothing," Daniel said, quickly putting it in his pocket.

You might think that was the end of it, but you don't know my brother when he's in a bad mood. He was only getting started. As soon as Mum left the room, our brother battle continued:

"I ain't messin' around, J – go back to Tissbury Primary where you belong!"

"Why should I? The Tigers is my team too now!"

"No, it ain't!"

"Yes, it is!"

"No, it ain't!"

"Okely-dokely, well let me see ... hmm ... yes, this is a tricksy one, isn't it?" Grandpa George said, leaning back in his chair and putting the really long fingers of his two really long hands together.

Whenever Mum and Dad got bored of our brotherly battles, they always sent us over to see Grandpa George. He was usually a pretty great peacemaker, but this time, he was "bamboozled". I had just finished my side of the story and now he needed a moment to "Hmm".

still trying to kick me out. It's not my fault that Craig found out we're brothers – it was Billy! And who cares anyway? The Tigers know now, and they still want me to be their assistant manager."

"Wait a wet weekend – the Tigers didn't know about the Barnstorming Ball Brothers?"

Uh-oh, I had forgotten that Grandpa George was in the room too. With an angry grunt and glare, Daniel snatched the ball back.

"Well, they do now, Grandpa..."

"But why did you try to hide that hobgoblin, Daniel? It sounds to me like Johnny is doing a simply spiffing job!"

My brother shrugged. "Yeah, he's doing all right, but like I said before, the Tigers is MY team. And how am I meant to flex my football skillz when he's always there, chatting silly on the side?"

"I'm just trying to help the team get better," I butted in, without the ball (again). "That's my job!"

"Nah, you're trying to help the other players get better, so that they get the glory instead of me!"

Wow, Daniel had got this sooooo wrong.

"Is this all because I didn't tell you about the Tiger Train? I'm sorry, I should ha—"

"Nah, I'm not bovvered about that playground prank…"

Well, he didn't look "not bovvered"! We had given up on the whole "only speak when you're holding the ball" thing, by the way.

"OK, well the reason I haven't been helping you is because you told me not to coach you EVER. Remember? That was Demand Number 5! Besides, you don't need me – you're already the best player in the team and everyone knows it!"

"Yeah, I KNOW, but…"

After that, there was this really awkward silence that felt like it went on for hours. At last, after a lot more "Hmm"ing, Grandpa George spoke up:

"Have I ever told you about the cranky Cotterley Cousins?"

"No, I don't think so." Daniel and I both shook our heads.

Grandpa George had so many stories that it was impossible to remember them all. Plus, he was so good at telling them that we never minded hearing them again.

"Well, I coached the cranky Cotterley Cousins for three years, between, let me see ... 1958 and 1961. They were both fabulous footballers – Don played on the right wing and Den on the left. For the first two years, everything was tickety-boo. But then one day, their mothers had a mahoosive mumble-jumble that turned into family fisticuffs. Over Christmas cards, of all things...

...Where was I? Oh yes, when the Cotterley Cousins turned up for training the next day, you could see the smoke smogging out of their ears. They were cranky at the best of times, but now they were cranky-doodle! They wouldn't say a winking word to each other, and they wouldn't pass the ball to each other either. Thanks to that tiff, we lost the next four games in a rabbity row!"

"So how did you stop it?" I asked.

"In the end, we called their mothers in, and they

told them off in front of the whole tiddly team! You should have seen Don and Den's faces – their cheeks were burning brighter than a boozy bonfire! Ho ho ho thankfully that was the end of that tiff. The Cotterley Cousins worked harder than ever – anything to stop their moody mummies from turning up at training again!"

Grandpa George was still chuckling loudly as he turned to my brother:

"So, Daniel, if you think having your little brother as your brazilliant assistant manager is embarrassing, you should shoving well think again!"

Thanks, Grandpa George! That wasn't the end of this tiff, but Daniel and I did agree to put it on a peace-pause for now. Because it was time for the Battling Ball Brothers to be barnstorming again. We had to find a way to work together and help the Tigers to win that league title. Without Mum and Dad making a scene in front of the whole team. Again.

CHAPTER 19

PROJECT "KEEP" CRAIG IN THE TEAM

On the way to the last Tigers training session of the season, I thought about some other really wise words that Grandpa George had said, waaaay back near the beginning of this story:

TIDDLYTASTIC new Tissbury Tigers Assistant Manager, it's your job to make the team work together, and to help that waster-of-spacer to waste less space!

So, how was I doing so far? Well, I gave myself a "B" for the teamwork part. The "pass, pass ... forwards pass, shoot!" against the Magpies, the first and last ten minutes against the Sloths, the Tiger Train against the Raptors – there were certainly signs of progress, even if Daniel still wasn't being totally teamy yet.

But the waster-of spacer part? I had to give myself a big fat "F" for that. Sorry, Grandpa George – "Project Craig" had been a flopping great failure so far.

"Project Talk to Craig" hadn't worked at all ... and neither had "Project Kick Craig Out" ... nor "Project Be Kind to Craig"/"Project Keep Craig Quiet" ... nor my latest attempt, "Project Keep Craig Up Front".

What was next – "Project Kidnap Craig"?

Just joking! I couldn't give up on completing Coach Crawley's second special task yet, though. No, no, no, because *TING! LIGHT-BULB MOMENT.* I HAD A SUPER-INCREDIBLE NEW IDEA!

Why hadn't I thought of it before? You see, so far, most of my projects had been about trying to stop Craig from causing trouble.

But that had only made things worse, and now everyone knew my terriBALL secret anyway (ha ha, geddit?). So what if, instead, I tried to actually help Craig become a better player (rather than just working on his throw-ins), or at least find a useful role for him in the team? I mean, that's what an assistant manager is meant to do, right, Grandpa George?!

It was time for ... "Project *KEEP* Craig in the Team". This one had to work; it just had to. First Daniel, and now Craig; hopefully by the time we kicked off against the Cobras, both of my big Tiger battles would be on peace-pause. At least until we won the league title, anyway. And then, hopefully, they would be over for ever.

"Have a lovely last practice, JB!"

"Have a lovely last practice, Coach! Actually, I had an idea—"

"Great, let's give it a go!"

"OK, well I thought we'd start with something FUN today," I announced. "Everyone loves a penalty shoot-out, yeah?"

"YEAH!" everyone replied. Daniel was even smiling a tiny, tiny bit.

"Good, so here are the teams:

TEAM 1: Noah, Jake, Connor, Finn, Temba

TEAM 2: Craig, Tyler, Reggie, Aroon, Daniel."

[Dev was missing again but Coach Crawley had made a deal with the drama teacher – no learning lines on the night before the big game. Hurray!]

"Nah, that ain't fair!" Daniel complained, just like I knew he would. "They've got a keeper and we haven't!"

"Isn't, Daniel," I thought to myself, but don't worry, I didn't say it! No, what I said was:

"You do have a keeper actually ... CRAIG!"

I thought Craig's shoulders would slump even lower when he heard his name, but no, he seemed to stand a bit straighter instead. Like a slightly happier walking lamp-post.

"Ha ha ha – good one," my brother carried on. "Fine, what I'm sayin' is, they've got a GOOD keeper and we ain't!"

"Well, let's just see how it goes," I said, handing Craig a pair of goalie gloves I'd ~~stolen~~ borrowed from the goalie glove shelf at home.

He didn't smile at me, or say anything polite or friendly, but there was definitely less of a frown on his forehead. Maybe my super-incredible new idea was going to work!

Beardy Jake decided to go first for Team 1. He took a really long run-up and then booted the ball as hard as he could ... straight at Craig. Here we go, this was it – his first go at being a goalkeeper...

The good news? Somehow, Craig did catch the ball as it came rocketing towards him.

The bad news? Beardy Jake's shot was so fierce that it sent him flying into the back of the net (with the ball still in his hands).

GOAL – 1–0!

Not a great start, and it got even worse when Noah saved Tyler's spot kick. Daniel didn't say anything, but I could guess what he was thinking:

Bro, why are you always tryna make me look BAD?

Come on, Craig! Could he do any better this time? No, ice-cold Connor placed his shot perfectly, just inside the post. The keeper had no chance.

GOAL – 2–0!

I made a quick note in my brain-book – "If Daniel ever gets injured, maybe Connor should be the back-up penalty taker?" – and then watched as Reggie smashed the ball top left bins with his lush left foot.

GOAL – 2–1!

Come on, Craig! I really needed him to stop this one, otherwise my super-incredible new idea was going to look super stupid.

Finn faked to go left, then aimed for bottom right bins instead. But he didn't hit it that hard, and it wasn't right in the corner like Connor and Reggie's strikes. Plus, like I told you before, Craig has really long, thin ruler legs. SAVED!

"Yes, Craig!" I heard Daniel clap and cheer like a proper team player. "Go on, Akintola!"

Aroon smiled and then fired an unstoppable shot into the top corner.

GOAL – 2–2!

We were down to the two Tigers strikers now. And what if both of them scored? Would Coach Crawley and I have to step up in sudden death? I was really, really hoping that wouldn't happen...

Temba walked all the way to the spot with the ball balanced on his boot, then dropped it down on the spot and took two steps back. It wasn't much of a run-up, but he still kicked it with plenty of power. **_BANG!_**

Craig dived low to his left, but the ball was going high to his right. It looked like a certain goal, but remember those really long, thin ruler legs? Well, it turns out they can almost touch the crossbar. SAVED!

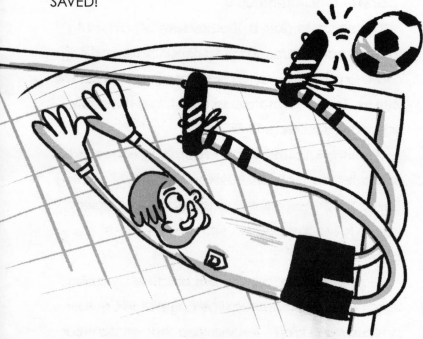

Wow, it was one of the best saves I had ever seen, and I wasn't even trying to be kind to Craig any more. Even he looked a little shocked at first, but then he beamed with pride.

"Fair play – that was a top stop, Craig!" Temba congratulated him. The more he talked, the more he showed what a top team player he was, and the more the others listened.

"Yes, you ledge!" Daniel punched the air.

Now, my brother just had to go up and...

GOAL – 3–2 to Team 2!

Daniel superstriker-celebrated like always, but then he turned around and pointed back at Craig, as if to say, "Yeah, you did something good too!" At last, my brother was starting to get the whole "we Tigers are a team" thing!

I, Johnny Ball: Undercover Football Genius, had a new greatest football achievement. Forget winning the County Cup – I had just turned Craig Crawley from a rubbish right-back into a pretty great goalkeeper!

You see, although Craig was officially a rubbish right-back, I'd wondered if he could play another position. Not striker –we had tried that already. But **TING!** I had realized he did have some of the skills you needed to be a good goalkeeper:

☉ He was tall.

☉ He could HOOF! the ball even further than Billy

(we could work on the accuracy later).

- ⚽ He could hurl it really hard too (remember the dodgeball during training? And that time I tried to teach Craig how to take a throw-in – he'd chucked it like a champion, so hard it had nearly went straight through me!).
- ⚽ He was good at stopping shots with his long, thin ruler legs (like against the Sloths, remember?).

If you're a nice person, you might be thinking, "Oh no, but what about Noah?" But don't worry, he was part of my plan too. In that horrible second half against the Sloths, he had been playing as a sweeper keeper, and it got me thinking a few things:

1) Noah is really fast.

2) Noah loves to tackle.

3) Noah should play right-back!

So you see, my idea was so super incredible that it made everyone happy. For the last league game against the Cobras, the Tigers would be playing with a new goalkeeper, a new right-back ... AND, as I was about to find out, a new manager too.

"Johnny, wait!" I heard a voice calling out at the end of training.

It was Coach Crawley.

"I just wanted to say thanks for all your hard work with Craig. It was so nice to see him doing well tonight, and that's why I won't be managing the Tigers any more."

WHAT? That didn't make sense!

"It's time for me and Craig to have some quality father-son time together. I want to cheer him on like the other parents and, who knows, maybe I'll even help train him up to be the next Nigel 'Hard Hands' Andrews!"

"But what about the Tigers?" I asked. "Who's going to manage them now?"

Coach Crawley laughed like the answer was really obvious. "You are, Johnny! Well, for our final game of the season, at least, and I know you're going to do an amazing job."

Wow, Tabia had been right all along; well kind of anyway:

...*Maybe he'll ask you to take over the Tigers because he's got to go to prison ... or on holiday to Hawaii...*

I didn't know what to say, so I said, "I don't know what to say, Coach."

"Just say that you're going to lead the Tigers to the league title."

"OK, I'm going to lead the Tigers to the league title."

"Good, that's the spirit! Well, off you go, Coach, and come up with a way to beat those Cobras."

CHAPTER 20

TAKING OVER THE TIGERS

JOHNNY BALL: TISSBURY TIGERS MANAGER – it sounded crazier than an aliens vs dinosaurs dance-off!

On the car journey home from training, I didn't say a single word. After my chat with Coach Crawley, I had a lot of things to think about. I could feel them circling around my head like loud helicopters. Things like:

Am I really good enough to be the new Tissbury Tigers Manager?

Am I really good enough to coach the Tigers to victory over the Cobras?

What are the players going to think when they find out?

And most urgent of all:

What is Daniel going to think when he finds out?

I was pretty sure that I knew the answer to that one: Daniel was going to have his BIGGEST AND LONGEST AND HORRIBLEST HUFF EVER. The timing was terrible, just when our brother battle was on a peace-pause, and just when he was finally acting more "teamy".

Could I just keep quiet about my new job until match day? No, that might make things even worse. At least if I told him now, with three days to go, Daniel might have calmed down by kick-off. I looked across the car at my brother, opened my mouth to speak ... and then sweet-chilli-chickened out.

"What are you waiting for, *ACUTE-ANGLE?*"

That was Tabia's voice in my head.

"This is no time to zip yer lips, laddy – it'll all come conkering out in the end!"

And that was Grandpa George (obviously).

I knew WHAT I needed to do, but HOW? Once we got home, I couldn't wait any longer.

KNOCK! KNOCK!

"Hello?"

"Yeah, what's up?" Daniel called through his bedroom door.

That was the sign that it was safe for me to enter. Phew! After his penalty-shoot-out win, he was in a pretty good mood … for now. Taking a deep breath, I opened the door and stepped inside.

"Daniel, I need to tell you something." I blurted it out like my mouth was on fire.

"It's better out than in, Johnny-bobbles!"

Great, now I had Mum in my head too!

Another deep breath, and then another big blurt: "Coach Crawley spoke to me after training, and he wants me to take over as Tigers manager for the Cobras match."

I shut my eyes and waited for Daniel to explode in a big (foot)ball of flames.

But weirdly, nothing happened – no shouting, no shoving, not even a knuckle crunch.

When I opened my eyes, my brother was just on his phone like always, typing really, really fast.

"It's no big deal, Bro," Daniel shrugged. "Coach Crawley was a flushed football manager, anyway."

Was that it? What about the fact that I, his supposedly shameful little brother, was taking over the Tigers?

"Just remember, yeah?" Daniel said, not even looking up from his phone screen. "You might be the team manager now, but you still ain't the boss of ME!"

That was the sign that it was time for me to leave him alone. Phew – well that had gone a whole lot better than I had expected!

On to my next challenge: telling Mum (and Dad, but mainly Mum).

"OH, JOHNNY-BUNNY, THAT'S JUST BRRRRILLLLIANT NEWS!" Mum squealed, jumping up and down as if she was trying to break a bed. I backed away, just to make sure that I was 121 per cent out of reach.

"Congratulations, champ, I knew you—" Dad started to say, but no, Mum was still squealing.

"We'll definitely need to get you a smart new coat now, won't we?"

"No, thanks – I already have my Tigers jacket."

"Yes, but that covers up your lovely little waistcoat! You have been wearing it underneath, haven't you?"

"Yes, Mum," I lied like a pro. (It was hidden in a secret box under my bed.)

"OK, well would you like a new hat as well?"

Hmm, maybe, but only something super stylish...

"How about one of those nice tweed flat caps?"

Nooooooooooo, I was a football manager, not a farmer! Besides, I had decided that I didn't want a

new football look after all. What was the point of
pretending to be someone else? I was doing a
pretty good job just being me, Johnny Ball: Tissbury
Tigers ~~Assistant~~ Manager.

"OK, darling, but if you change your mind—"

"I won't!"

Telling Mum the news was basically the same
as shouting it out in the street through a massive
megaphone. Straight away, she was on her phone,
inviting everyone along to "Johnny's big day".

Grandpa George, Miss Patel, Tabia and her
whole entire family, someone I'd never even heard
of called "Helen"...

Thanks, Mum, as if I needed any more pressure on
my nine-and-a-quarter-year-old shoulders!

Because I still had some very important teenagers
left to tell: the Tigers. How would they feel about me
being their new manager – "calm" or "cranked"?
What if they walked off and refused to play? What if
Craig thought I had stolen his dad's job?

There was only one way to find out, but telling the
Tigers would have to wait until – da a daaaa –OUR
FINAL FACE-OFF AGAINST ... THE COBRAS!

CHAPTER 21

CHANGE OF PLAN, CHANGE OF SHAPE

TISSBURY TIGERS VS COOPERSTON COBRAS (PART I)

It turns out I was worrying over nothing.

"Congrats, J, that's JUICY!"

"Cool, we're deffo gonna crush those Cobras now!"

"So, what's the wonder-plan, Coach?"

Good question, Beardy Jake! We were in a Tiger team huddle, with twenty minutes to go until kick-off against the Cobras. This was it – the final face-off. We knew WHAT we had to do – win! No draws no losses – we needed all three points to overtake the Cobras in the table. Only if we did that would the league title be ours.

But HOW were we going to win? Well, that was my job now, as the Tissbury Tigers manager. I was already feeling super nervous, so I started with something easy – the team line-up:

What next? Oh yeah, talk some more about
TEAMWORK, Johnny!

"If we're going to win the league title today, we're
going to have to work hard and we're going to have
to work TOGETHER. So no huffs, and no selfish heroes!
Remember the Tiger Train against the Raptors? When
we play like a top team, we win like a top team!"

Now for the next, more difficult bit:

"Daniel, this is for you," I said, handing him a super-
cool new armband, with "C" on one side and "DB9"
on the other. (Thanks, Mum!) "You're our top scorer
but you're also our team captain. If things get tough
out there today, we're going to need you to lead!"

"Slick!" my brother replied, proudly putting it on.
"Time to lift that title, Tigers!"

Right, we were ready for kick-off, and so were the lots and lots and lots of supporters who had come along to watch my big day. (Not-so-thanks, Mum!)

"JOHNNY-BOSS'S TIGER-STRIPED ARMY!"

"Here we go, laddies, let's topple those lob-shots!"

"Good luck, *PIE-CHART!*"

Arghh, there were family and best friends everywhere! This time, I needed something waaaay bigger than a hand to hide behind... *TING! LIGHT-BULB MOMENT* –Grandpa George's extra-long scarf!

Perfect, now I could focus on the football. Come on you Tigers!

Out on the pitch, it would be a battle between the league's two best teams, and on the touchline,

I was going brain-to-brain with another football genius. Pedro Bolsa, the Cobras manager, was famous for being a) very successful and b) a little bit … strange. He didn't use "playground prankz" to win football matches (like the old me), but "Peculiar Pedro" did use them to turn his players into TOTAL FITNESS FREAKS.

Late-night litter pick-ups, water fights wearing heavy army back-packs, relay races across hot coals – those were just some of the things that Pedro made his team do, apparently. Whether that was true or not, the Cobras were all amazing athletes who didn't stop moving all match long.

"It's a pleasure to meet you, Mr Ball," Pedro said as we met near the halfway line. Even though it was a pretty nice day, he was wearing one of the biggest, thickest coats I had ever seen. Maybe it was a scarf fat-suit, I dunno…

"Pleasure to meet you too, Mr Bolsa," I replied.

Instead of shaking my hand, the Cobras manager elbowed my elbow, and then took a seat on an upside-down bucket that he had brought with him. As I said before, a little bit … strange.

Right, game time! What the Tigers needed was

a strong start, but instead, we gave the Cobras a one-goal head start. In the third minute, a cross came into the box, Craig lifted up his really long arms to catch the ball … and dropped it … right at their striker's feet. Tap-in – 1–0!

As I watched in horror, a flood of silly football phrases rushed through my head:

Butter fingers!

What a howler!

He's dropped a clanger there!

Dodgy keeper!

What was the manager thinking?

YOU DON'T KNOW WHAT YOU'RE DOING! YOU DON'T KNOW WHAT YOU'RE DOING!

The Tigers are really on the back foot now…

Oh no, had giving Craig the goalie gloves actually been my new worst football idea ever? His shoulders were starting to slump already.

"Unlucky, son!" ~~Coach~~ Mr Crawley called out cheerfully from behind the goal. "We all make mistakes..."

Yes, but not in the first few minutes of a huge, final face-off!

I looked over at my angry brother on the halfway line. He was clenching his fists so hard they were turning white. Uh-oh, this was a massive test for him. As captain, Daniel could either make things much better or much, much worse. It just depended how teamy he was feeling. I tried my best to send him a mind-message: "Please don't shout at Crai—"

I could see my brother opening his mouth to let out something really mean, but at the last second,

he looked down at his armband and decided to clap instead.

COME ON, HEADS UP —
THERE'S LOADSA TIME LEFT!

Phew – nice one, Bro! It wasn't over yet. We were still in the game.

As soon as the match restarted, the Tigers raced forward on the attack. Finn and Aroon were dominating in midfield, but once again, they just couldn't find that killer pass through to our star strike force. The Cobras were just so quick and clever. It was like playing against an army of ants, not eleven humans – they were everywhere! Every time we tried a through-ball, one of their defenders beat Daniel or Temba to the ball. It was 2 vs 2 back there and, so far, the Cobras centre-backs looked faster, bigger and stronger.

Think, Johnny, think!

Soon, it would be half-time, and what was I going to say in my team talk? I knew that it was going to take more than just a Coach Crawley "Keep going!" to out-manage Pedro and lead the Tigers to the league title. But what? Talent + teamwork + ... tactics!

TING! LIGHT-BULB MOMENT.

You see, when I wasn't busy thinking up great football ideas, I had been working hard on my Maths skillz with Tabs. At first, I used to just sit there in class, thinking:

"YAWN! What's the point of all these annoying numbers?"

But then one day, Miss Patel showed us how you could use Maths to solve problems in THE REAL WORLD! And suddenly, it all made so much sense. If I got really good at Maths, I could even use it on THE FOOTBALL FIELD!

Our 2 strikers were struggling to score against their 2 centre-backs. So how could we solve that problem? By adding an extra attacker – 3 vs 2!

CHANGE OF PLAN – CHANGE OF SHAPE! And what shape would make it super difficult for the Cobras defenders? A TRIANGLE!

I had seen Paul Porterfield use one lots of times when Tissbury Town needed a goal. Maths to the rescue! As soon as the half-time whistle went, I got straight to work:

"Right, Tigers, it's time for a tactical switch! Forget 4-4-2; we're swapping to a 4-3-3 now. So in midfield, it'll be Dev, Finn and Aroon. Then Reggie and Temba, you'll play just behind Daniel. OK?"

There were a few cool-kid nods, but mostly just confused faces. So I drew a picture of our new formation in my "pocket" notebook:

"OK?"

"Yeah, that's a swipe system, Coach!"

"Ah, gotcha – that's golden!"

"You've got big brains for a lil boy, Boss!"

Thanks, Tyler! It was nice to know that my players were impressed, but only one thing really mattered now: was the Tissbury Tigers Triangle actually going to work?

CHAPTER 22

TIGERS FOR THE TITLE

TISSBURY TIGERS VS COOPERSTON COBRAS (PART 2)

Of course the Tissbury Tiger Triangle worked – duh! You didn't doubt my football genius, did you?

Finn's first touch in the second half was a forward pass through to Reggie, who had snuck into his new inside-left role without our opponents noticing. [Take that, Pedro!]

ZING – TIGERS TRIANGLE ACTIVATED!

ZING – COBRAS CENTRE-BACKS OUTNUMBERED!

It was 3 of us against 2 of them, and we were getting closer and closer to the enemy goal...

When the first defender dived in, Reggie passed it across to Temba, who controlled the ball beautifully on the top of his boot.

The second Cobras centre-back was already racing towards him, and he was as tall and wide and solid as a wall. Uh-oh, how was Temba going to get the ball past him? No problem, with a fancy flick of his right boot, he scooped the ball straight over the defender's head and it dropped down perfectly for Daniel to volley in. *BANG!* – 1–1!

Yes, yes, yes, what a goal! We were back in the game, and it was all thanks to Maths – and Temba, Reggie and my brother, of course ... oh, OK, AND ME! With our new Tissbury Tigers Triangle, it was as easy as 1, 2, 3 ... *GOAL!*

While Captain Daniel celebrated with his teammates for once, I raced over to thank Tabia for making me go back to the Tigers, and for helping me with my homework.

"No problem, *SET-SQUARE*," she cheered. "That's what best friends are for!"

Now, if we could just score one more goal, we could win the league title, and I would have a second trophy to go with my County Cup. Come on! But before I could get too carried away, we had some serious defending to do...

The problem with having one more Tiger in attack was that it meant we had one less Tiger in midfield. My players were all working so hard together, but with a few fast one-touch passes, our creative opponents cut straight through them like a sword through jelly.

Uh-oh, DANGER ALERT – COBRAS ON THE COUNTER-ATTACK!

Too late. After some silky skillz, their striker sprinted between Tyler and Beardy Jake and then into the Tigers penalty area. Now the only thing between him and the winning goal was ... Craig!

It was a massive moment – for the Tigers, and for me, their new manager. I held my breath as the Cobras striker pulled his leg back and fired a fierce shot towards the bottom corner. **BANG!**

I watched in agony as the ball cannoned off his boot ... and swerved through the air ... towards the top corner ... to win the title for the Cobras...

Great big BUT (hehehe!), that's the last one, I promise! – at the last second, Craig stretched out his really long, thin ruler right leg and somehow flicked it just round the post for a corner. SAVED!

"Wow, well done, son!" Mr Crawley cheered. I had never seen anyone look so proud.

Things I never ever thought I would say EVER:

1) Maths to the rescue.

2) Craig Crawley to the rescue.

But it was true; our new Number 1 had really saved us.

"Yes, you ledge!" Daniel yelled out as he raced back into the box to defend the corner. For one silly second, I thought he was even going to hug Craig. But no, a quick fist bump was enough emotion for one day.

"Excellent work, Craig!" I shouted out, once I had recovered from the shock of what I'd just seen. "Come on, Tigers – only five minutes to go!"

There were actually seven minutes left, but I wanted to panic my players a bit. It's a classic Paul Porterfield trick.

"Only five?" Daniel replied just like I'd hoped he would. "Right, time to turn it up, Tigers!"

And time for me to out-brain my opponent. I looked over at Peculiar Pedro, who seemed super confident as he sat there on his upside-down bucket, and then out onto the pitch. Could I come up with one last great football idea to win the league title? I was searching for clues, searching for space...

TING! MEGA LIGHT-BULB MOMENT – it was a plan that even Paul Porterfield himself would have been super pleased with.

In order to stop the Tissbury Tigers Triangle, the Cobras left-back was now marking Temba, and following him wherever he went. That meant that whenever Temba moved away from the wing and into the centre, there was this big gap where the Cobras left-back was supposed to be.

Pedro must have spotted it, but maybe he thought his team was speedy enough to defend anything. Or maybe he thought he was up against a clueless nine-and-a-quarter-year-old kid. Well, whatever, he thought WRONG! So, which Tiger was going to fill that gap?

Dev? No, even without the all-night line-learning, he was still looking really tired.

Noah? Of course! He had so much speed and so much energy too. There was no way that the Cobras would be able to cope with someone that rapid. It was time for...

ATTACK OF THE FLYING FULL-BACK PART 2: RIGHT WING, RIGHT TIME!

The next time he came over to take a throw-in, I showed Noah the plan. I even decorated it with circles and arrows to make everything super clear.

"Yeah, sick plan, J!" he said with a smile.

Excellent, we were all set for "Attack of the Flying Full-back Part 2". Well, almost – I had something to say to my brother first. You'll see in a second...

Right – ready! As soon as Temba made his next move towards the middle, I shouted "GO!" and Noah sprinted into that left-back gap like there was a cheetah chasing after him. Now all he needed was the ball...

Dev spotted the run and played the perfect pass. **PING!** Noah was away, with lots of defenders trailing behind him and only the goal (and the goalkeeper) in front of him!

But before you stop reading and start celebrating a Tigers title victory, there's one thing you need to remember about Noah – for a long time, he was our goalkeeper. He was good at kicking, catching, jumping and tackling – but shooting? Not so much.

When he got to the edge of the penalty area, Noah had a full-on football freeze. He had never been so far forward! What was he supposed to do now? It was like he was a robot who had run out of instructions.

No, no, no, the Cobras were catching up! If Noah didn't do something soon, our best chance would be wasted.

"SHOOT!" shouted every Tigers player and supporter.

Except one:

"PASS!" Daniel called out as he burst into the box like a classic superstriker. That's right – this time, my brother was part of the plan. In fact, he was about to be the hero!

But as the ball rolled towards him, my brother pulled back his right leg and ... *WHACK!*

"Owwwww!" Daniel screamed out as he fell to the floor.

One of the Cobras centre-backs had hacked him down horribly, just as he was about to win the

title for Tissbury. I was too shocked to even shout, "Referee!" That didn't matter, though, because it was the most obvious red card ever, and a penalty too. But who was going to take it?

I rushed over to see how Daniel was – it didn't look good.

"I've got this," he managed to say between big gasps of pain. Then he got up slowly and hobbled over to put the ball on the spot. He looked like Dad with his dodgy right ankle.

Really? Daniel could hardly walk, let alone take a title-winning penalty! This was waaaay too important to be messing around. Yes, he was the captain, but I was the manager! I had to stop him...

"Daniel, I don't think—"

"I'm fine."

Be brave, Johnny, be brave!

"No, you're not – you're injured! I know you really want to be the hero here, but be a captain instead and think about your teammates. They don't deserve to lose the title just because you're too selfish to say that you can't kick the ball."

"I can!"

"No, you can't! I'm the manager and it's my decision. Connor, you're taking it instead!"

Wow, can you believe I said all that? I can't! But at that moment, it was like someone else was speaking for me – a much older, wiser football genius, who was brave enough to make the big decisions, even when family was involved.

"Just so ya know, Bro," Daniel ranted in a rage, "if this gets grilled, I'm never gonna forgive you!"

"Well, let's just see how it goes," I said calmly, handing the ball to Connor.

I thought that Daniel might keep ranting and raging until I finally gave in, but the captain inside him must have told him to stop and have a quiet huff instead.

"Wait a minute – what's going on?" I heard Dad cry out on the touchline. "This is RIDICULOUS! Why isn't Daniel taking it?"

Oh no, not another embarrassing family fight...

"Steven, calm down! Can't you see that Danny-doo-doo's hurt? He can't take it!"

"Hmmph, I suppose so..."

Thanks, Mum! Right, time for a BIG CONNOR CONFIDENCE BOOST.

"Good luck, you've got this!" I told him.

"Yeah, Connor, you're the spot-kick king!" added "Temba the team player" (I had updated my brain-book).

Even though he was one of our best players, he didn't mind someone else getting the glory. In a top team, everyone trusts each other, don't they? Temba and I totally trusted Connor to win us the title, even if my brother didn't. Come on!

As he placed the ball down on the spot, the Cobras keeper tried to put him off by wasting time and saying silly, mean things. But Connor wasn't listening; he was in his own ice-cold world.

FWEEEET! When the referee blew his whistle, Connor ran up and **BANG!** He placed his shot perfectly, just inside the post, just like in training. The Cobras keeper guessed the right way, but he couldn't even get a glove-tip on the ball.

GOOOOOOOOOOOOAAAAAAAALLLLLLLLLLLLLLLL!!!

2–1 to the Tigers! Connor raced over to the corner

flag and dived across the grass. Soon, he was at the bottom of a big pile of players ... oh and one super-excited manager. How did I get there so fast? With another running knee slide, of course! Because now the Tigers were only two minutes away from winning the league title!

"Sweet spot kick, mate," Daniel said, doing a very long and complicated "handshake" with Connor. "I knew you'd flame it. Now let's keep it tight, yeah, Tigers!"

My brother was all smiles and no huff now that he could see the trophy at the end of the tunnel. We had our captain back ... and just in time! Daniel couldn't really run any more, but he could definitely shout football phrases:

"Man on, Finn!

Get goal-side of him, Tyler!

Watch the overlap, Reggie!"

For those last two minutes, Daniel was basically me, but out on the pitch. Yes, the Barnstorming Ball Brothers were back together!

It felt like aaaages, but eventually the final whistle went. We had done it – we had won the league title!

"TIGERS! TIGERS! TIGERS!"

"Noooooo!" Peculiar Pedro groaned. It must have really hurt, being out-managed by a rival football genius. Sorry! The Cobras boss was so upset that he picked up his bucket and put it over his head.

"Congratulations, Mr Ball," he mumbled from under his strange new hat.

After that, everything was a blur for a bit. For a second, I thought I was so happy that I was actually floating on air, but no, the players were lifting me up to take me on a lap of honour around the field.

"JOHNNY! JOHNNY! JOHNNY!"

From up high, I had the perfect view of the title celebrations below. It turns out my great football ideas can bring a lot of happiness to a lot of people: my friends – not just Tabia, but some of the other Tissbury Primary players – my family and, of course, my team.

"JOHNNY! JOHNNY! JOHNNY!"

I won't lie to you – as the Tigers chanted my name, I cried (just a few!) tears of joy. What an adventure it had been ... already! I was so proud of all my players, and I was pretty proud of myself too. Despite all the difficult moments, my dream was still alive: I was on the way to becoming "THE NEXT PAUL PORTERFIELD", the future number one football genius in the whole wide world.

"Err … Johnny?" I heard a voice say when the Tigers dropped me back down on the pitch.

It was Craig, and he looked … friendly, like his dad.

"Soz for being so harsh before – you know, calling you 'waistcoat weirdo' and telling everyone who you really were and all that…"

Thanks for the reminder, Craig!

"…it's because I thought you were trying to kick me off the team, but I was well wrong about that. You're class. Cheers for believing in me, Boss!"

You're welcome! It's weird; when you help your team win a trophy, suddenly you turn into a very popular person. As I was talking to Tabia, I heard my name again, well part of it anyway:

"Err … J…?"

It was Daniel. "Look, my bad, Bro," he said, pulling me into a cool-kid hug (always one shoulder, NEVER two). "You were spot on about that spot-kick, and I'm soz about the way I've been acting. I'm gonna make it up to ya – watch this…"

Uh-oh, what was Daniel about to do?

"Listen up, Tigers!" he clapped like a proper

captain. "Top work today, everyone – we're the Championz, innit! Soz, I know I haven't always been his number one fan, but I want to say a big up to my lil bro, the coolest coach around. Take a bow, JOHNNY BALL!"

"HIP HIP ⋯ HURRAY!"

Beardy Jake was lifting me up on his big, strong shoulders…

"HIP HIP ⋯ HURRAY!"

Then together the Tigers were throwing me high into the sky…

"HIP HIP ⋯ HURRAY!"

And, thankfully, catching me when I came back down again.

"Actually, I've got something to say too." It was Dev. As everyone turned, he took a deep breath and ... "I'm inescoply."

"What?"

Dev said it again, and not into his shirt this time. "I'm in the school play. Just in case, you know, you wanted to come and see it ... or whatever."

Just when the silence was starting to get super awkward, Beardy Jake spoke up. "Cool, man, why didn't you say before? When does it start?"

"Yeah, and do we get teammate's rates?" The rest of the Tigers couldn't wait.

Phew, what a day! And Daniel hadn't finished being nice to me yet. After we'd all collected our winners' medals, it was time for the Tissbury Tigers captain to lift the league trophy.

"Bro, get over 'ere!" Daniel called out to me. "I'm gonna need your help holding this bling thing up high!"

Yes, Johnny Ball: Undercover Football Genius had worked out well for both of us in the end. Grandpa George had got it right (again) – the football world had better watch out for Daniel and me ... the Barnstorming Ball Brothers!

MATCH REPORT 6

JNB

TISSBURY TIGERS 2–1 COOPERSTON COBRAS

STARTING LINE-UP (MARKS OUT OF 10):
Craig 10, Noah 10, Connor 10, Beardy Jake 10, Tyler 10, Finn 10, Aroon 10, Dev 10, Reggie 10, Temba 10, Daniel 10

SCORERS:
Daniel, Connor

WHAT WENT WELL:
1) We won the league title!!!!
2) The Tigers played like a proper team
3) Daniel played like a proper captain (well, mostly)
4) Craig played like a proper keeper
5) I showed everyone that I'm not just a lil boy with a big football brain

EVEN BETTER IF:
Right now, I can't think of ANYTHING at all!

ACKNOWLEDGEMENTS

The dream team has done it again! Massive "Thank You!"s go to:

1) My editor, Daisy Jellicoe, who worked her magic on my messy ideas once more.

2) Laurissa Jones, for all her design flair.

3) Tim Wesson, whose illustrations are, as Johnny would say, "super incredible".

4) Nick Walters, agent and champion.

And...

5) Everyone else who has supported me and my books: family, friends, authors, teachers, booksellers, librarians and, of course, readers. I'm for ever grateful to you all.

*YOUR FAVOURITE FOOTBALL GENIUS STARS
IN HIS FIRST ADVENTURE!*

"Funny and entertaining. Perfect for fans of
Ultimate Football Heroes."
Tom Palmer, author of Football Academy

"A fantastic book and it blew my mind."
Toppsta reader review

"Written with great style and humour."
The School Librarian

"A match winner... Laugh-out-loud moments from
kick-off to final whistle."
Amazon reader review

BY THE AUTHOR OF ULTIMATE FOOTBALL HEROES

JOHNNY BALL

ACCIDENTAL FOOTBALL GENIUS

MATT OLDFIELD

ILLUSTRATED BY
TIM WESSON

ABOUT THE AUTHOR

Matt Oldfield loves football. He loves playing football, watching football, reading about football, but most of all, he loves writing about football for kids. With his brother, Tom, he has written the bestselling Ultimate Football Heroes series of playground to pitch biographies. He won the *Telegraph* Children's Sports Book of the Year for *Unbelievable Football: The Most Incredible True Football Stories*. Johnny Ball is his first fiction series.

Credits

Front cover: © Bevis Boobacca/Corbis

Back cover: © Jakub Semeniuk/iStockphoto.com, © Royalty-Free/Corbis, © agencyby/iStockphoto.com, © Andy Cook/iStockphoto.com, © Christopher Ewing/iStockphoto.com, © zebicho – Fotolia.com, © Geoffrey Holman/iStockphoto.com, © Photodisc/Getty Images, © James C. Pruitt/iStockphoto.com, © Mohamed Saber – Fotolia.com